Additional Book by A&E Kirk

Divinicus Nex Chronicles

Demons at Deadnight
https://www.amazon.com/Demons-Deadnight-Paranormal-Divinicus-Chronicles-ebook/dp/B006UKMMU0/

Drop Dead Demons
https://www.amazon.com/Drop-Dead-Demons-Paranormal-Chronicles-ebook/dp/B00KKYL62C/

Demons in Disguise
https://www.amazon.com/Demons-Disguise-Paranormal-Divinicus-Chronicles-ebook/dp/B019H2KUSI/

Paranormal Poisons Saga

Midnight Poison
https://www.amazon.com/Midnight-Poison-Fantasy-Thriller-Paranormal-ebook/dp/B01MU2HX2J/

Interview with a Hex Boy

A&E Kirk

DEDICATION

To both the Super Fans and the blogging ladies who
mercilessly grilled The Boys. And special thanks to Izzy
Crusoe for helping put it all together!

THE HEX BOY INTERVIEWS

Get ready for some Hextraordinary fun!

We've consolidated all the interviews that those sexy Hex Boys did with bloggers on our past blog tours PLUS there is new content. In the DIVINICUS NEX CHRONICLES, Ayden, Matthias, Jayden, Blake, Tristan, and Logan are the hunkalicious team who use supernatural powers to battle the most dangerous paranormal monsters on the planet, but in this book, they take on even more powerful creatures. Their Fans! Yes indeed, The Boys answer new questions received directly from the ultimate Hex Boy lovers. Ready to see how they do? Then read on and enjoy!

Yours as Always, With Hugs and Gratitude,

A & E Kirk

AEKIRK.com
Facebook.com/AandEKirk

MATTHIAS

Host: Melissa at Books and Things

Oh, since many of you know that I love those Hex boys from *Demons at Deadnight* and made them a special room in my harem (which is untouchable by me UNTIL their 21st b-day *waggles eyebrows*. Well, I noticed that several of you gravitated toward Matthias. So, I decided to try to shed some light on this mysterious individual. Surprisingly, he said YES to an interview so I jumped right on it (now, now... he's still a youngin'... *mumbles* dirty minded peeps..).

Melissa: Thanks for agreeing to the interview. Okay, *clears throat* I guess I'll start with an easy question. If you could pick a power what would it be?

Matthias: I'd prefer no power at all. But if I could choose, I'd like the power to heal others. Or time travel.

Melissa: Really? That is so sweet! I'd really like....

Slamming doors outside gives way to arguing.

Matthias: *Scrutinizes Melissa suspiciously.* You expecting company?

Melissa: *Gives wide eyed innocent look* No. Um... let's just keep going with the interview, shall we? Um... What do you like about your power and what do you dislike?

Matthias: In my line of work it gives me the upper hand when it comes to stealth and attack. I don't like that it can be dangerous to innocents. Every power can be hazardous when misused or misunderstood. Aurora is a classic example of that—

Front door opens.

Melissa looks confused

Blake: Hey dude!

Matthias: *Groans.*

Logan: *Pulls uselessly on Blake's arm.* He's going to kill us.

Matthias: *Lights flicker.* Too easy, mate. Torture is a much more viable option.

Melissa: *Looks suddenly confused at the flickering lights.*

Blake: Jayden said you were doing an interview, we came to make sure you didn't give us a bad rep. *Takes Melissa's hand and bows to kiss her knuckles.* Good day, Mi'lady.

Melissa: *blushes and then reminds herself he's too young* *squirms in chair*

Matthias: *Shoves Blake away.* I don't give us a bad rep.

Logan: Aurora thought we were kidnapping killers.

Matthias: Did I ask for your input?

Melissa: *sighs* Hey guys? Let's get back to the interview. Matthias, how do you feel about Aurora?

Blake: She's the sexiest thing to walk the Earth. Well, second sexiest. *Winks at Melissa.*

Melissa: *Eyebrows raise*

Logan: *Rolls eyes.*

Matthias: *Frowns* Aurora should move to a remote island where she's never seen, heard, or spoken of ever again. Somewhere she can't cause any more damage.

Blake: Whoa, it's sad how in love with her you are—

Melissa: *mouth turns into an "O"*

Matthias: What?!

Melissa: *Snaps mouth shut*

Blake: —since Aurora's in love with me.

Logan: *Shakes head.* You're not even listening to the conversation, are you?

Melissa: Okay, let's get back to the interview, shall we? Um, about Aurora... this may kill you to say, but what is her best attribute? Her worst?

Blake: Her best—

Logan: *Smacks Blake.*

Melissa: *Snickers*

Matthias: I'll admit *strangling noise* an admirable quality is that she'll do anything for her family. And your second question? Her ability to muck-up everything. Especially our team. We worked fine before. Now we have people breaking rules, lying, naming missions, questioning my authority. This list goes on. But the worst is her thinking she's part of our team. She's an absolute loon. And a bloody thief!

Logan: Ayden said she borrowed—

Blake: *Snorts laughter* Yeah, if borrowed means steal right from under your nose. Man, that was smooth.

Matthias: That wasn't smooth! She's messed with all your brains. She's reckless. Stubborn as hell too. Even if she'll die, she'll stick to whatever idiotic plan she came up with.

Logan: *Nods*

Blake: I like to think she's just delightfully determined.

Matthias: You also like to think you're intelligent.

Melissa: *Rubs neck from the back and forth convo* *AHEM* What is your greatest wish? Do you think it is possible?

Matthias: For Aurora to disappear, forever. And with my dad as sheriff, anything is possible.

Melissa: *Eyes widen*

Blake: Come on, dude. Gotta be honest.

Room darkens.

Matthias: *Clenches fists.* Sorry. I didn't mean to be dismissive. The truth is I don't want Aurora gone because her family would miss her and I wouldn't wish that on anyone. Just gone from my life would be nice. *Clears throat.* And while I mean no disrespect, I'm not prepared to share my greatest wish. Although I will tell you that it's impossible.

Melissa: **Sighs* *Taps pencil on notebook thinking of the next question**

Blake: **Wiggles eyebrows at Melissa.** Want to know my greatest wish?

Matthias: She doesn't. No one does.

Melissa: Not until you are 21...

Blake: That you'll give me your number. **Grins.** And its possibility depends entirely upon you, my dazzling beauty.

Logan: She asked for Matthias. Not you. You're just lucky she's nice enough to let you stay.

Blake: She's just playing hard to get. And Melissa, if you want to bring a friend on our date, Logan can come too.

Logan: **Squeaks.** No, no. Uh. **Blushes. Clears throat.** Can't make it. Got a...thing.

Melissa: **Laughs** Matthias, I have seen many girls swoon over your future picture. So... tell me... what would you like in a girl? What makes you take notice?

Matthias: What picture?

Melissa: Um....

Blake: I told Logan not to send those nude photos of you.

Logan: What?!

Melissa: **Giggles**

Matthias: **Shakes head** You're idiots. **Takes deep breath. Faces Melissa.**Confidence, quiet confidence makes me take notice. Not shy, just not an ear-basher. Intelligent, driven, independent, and she has to like the classics.

Blake: Since when are you into cars?

Matthias: Wuthering Heights, Othello, Macbeth, The Odyssey.

Blake: Ever heard of those models, Logan? I haven't.

Matthias: *Hangs head.*

Logan: Think Shakespeare. You've got to start paying attention in English.

Melissa: Don't worry Blake, classic cars are the best. Think of a Charger.*Hands picture* Now, maybe we can get back to the interview. Matthias, anything that surprises you about yourself?

Blake: You mean other than he hasn't dumped Aurora's body in the lake yet?

Matthias: Don't be stupid. There'd be no body to find.

Logan: *Mutters.* Kidnapping killers...

Matthias: Shut it, mate. I've already admitted I don't really want her dead. But fantasy is good for the soul.

Blake: I've got a fantasy involving whipped cream—

Melissa: *Mumbles.* Well, that car picture didn't last long...

Matthias: Enough!

Logan: You don't even like whipped cream.

Matthias: I'm surprised I haven't murdered these morons.

Blake: Dude, we're family.

Matthias: *Freezes.*

Blake: Like brothers.

Matthias: *Looks stricken.* Bugger.

Melissa: *Looks awed.*

Logan: I think he looks surprised. Which may answer your question, Miss Melissa.

Blake: Group hug!

Matthias: *Raises warning fist.* Eyes on, hands off.

Blake: That's all right, you and Logan weren't even part of the group.

Melissa: *Looks flustered.*

Matthias: *Stands between Blake and Melissa.* Like I said.

Melissa: *Tries to change the subject quickly.* One last question: Who is Bubbles and why did you help her out? *Grins*

Matthias: *Turns to Melissa, keeping a wary eye on Blake.* Bubbles is Selena's best friend. Selena's five and despite the hindrance of having Aurora as her sister, she's all right.

Blake: Oh, come on. You adore Selena.

Melissa: ...and you are adorable with her...

Matthias: Point is she and Bubbles shouldn't suffer for Aurora's incompetence.

Logan: That's not fair because technically Bubbles' problems were our fault—

Matthias: If you like Aurora so much, go annoy her!

Blake: *Points to Melissa.* Why would we leave a goddess like—

Matthias and Logan: Shut up, Blake!

Matthias: Thank you for your time Melissa. Please ignore any communication from Blake that might get past me. It's for your own safety. And sanity. If we're done, I'd be more than happy to escort these idiots out of here.

Blake: *Getting forced out the door by Matthias.* Did I mention I was eighteen?!

Melissa: *Snorts.*

Logan: She said you had to be twenty-one.

Blake: *Gripping the door frame.* I'm twenty-one!

Wind rushes through the room. Blake ducks out as door slams shut.

Melissa: Well, that was an interview, wasn't it? *Sighs.* So, how long do I have to wait for all of them to be 21??? *Shakes thought from head.*

Well, that was Matthias... and Blake with Logan. *Grins* I hope you enjoyed my little chat with the boys. However, remember, they are all off limits to everyone here... and only off limits for a few more years for me. :D

BLAKE

Host: Jen at Jen's Book Closet

Welcome, welcome! I'm so glad you all could join us today for my interview of Blake from DEMONS AT DEADNIGHT. For all of you who've read the book, you know Blake...tall, rock solid, sexy as hell...well, he may be an extravagant flirt, but it's no biggie because so am I and I just don't think Blake's met his match! :D On to the interview!!

Jen: To start this interview out right, I need to know 2 very important things, Blake: 1-favorite books and 2-favorite cupcake? (this could make or break our relationship Blake)

Blake: You get me alone and all you want to do is ask—Wait. Relationship? Yes! *Fist pumps air*

Shadows sneak up behind Blake

Blake: Don't worry babe, I won't lose you. My favorite books are Bond. James Bond. Did you know they were books first? I thought Logan was pulling my leg. But there they are, all Bond's lady techniques written down for me to study. Which brings me to my next point, you could put my lips to much better use than talking.

Ayden: Yeah, like duck-taping them shut.

Blake: *Whirls.* Hey! This is a private party. Right, babe?

Matthias: You crashed my interview, thought I'd return the favor.

Jen: He does have a point, Blake. *pats Blake on the back*

Ayden: And I thought I'd make sure you don't give us a bad rep.

Blake: Me? What about Matthias?!

Ayden: Matthias only makes people think we're murders. *You* make people think we're hormonal maniacs.

Jen: *Questioning look at Ayden* How is that worse? *confused*

Blake: *Looks pleadingly at Jen* You can kick them out. Don't let them ruin our date, babe!

Jen: Don't worry, Ayden *bats eyes at boys* I like bad boys. Blake, they'll behave, I'm sure of it. *pats Blakes hand* Besides, I like a crowd. *winks at boys*

Matthias: *Pulls up chair next to Blake* Hmm, doesn't look like she wants us gone.

Ayden: And why would she? I'm smokin' hot.

Jen: *stares at intently at Ayden with mouth hanging open*

Matthias: *Scowls at Ayden* You've really let that go to your head.

Blake: Jen is clearly Team Blake, which is why I'm not threatened by you being here. Babe, my favorite cupcakes...*Winks*...are yours.

Matthias: **Punches Blake's arm.**

Jen: **owl eyes** What? What just happened?

Ayden: **Smacks Blake upside head.** I can't believe you just said that!

Blake: What? No! **Shoves both boys back** She bakes! Cupcakes. Real cupcakes!

Matthias and Ayden: What?

Blake: Jayden made her chocolate peanut butter cupcakes last week.

Jen: **smiles crazily** He did?

Matthias: Oh. **Grumbles unintelligibly and stares at floor.**

Ayden: That was her recipe? They were delicious. Well...umm. **Shifts uncomfortably and looks anywhere, but at Jen** We thought you meant—never mind.

Jen: **Winks at Ayden** No worries, hun.

Blake: They were awesome, by the way, chick-a-dee. But I think you should come over to my place tonight and bake some just so I can compare against Jayden's. We can watch a movie after. I like to cuddle.

Jen: I'm down! I really want to try to make a banana cream cupcake with filling and whip cream topper. And, I *love* movies...and cuddling! Although, is it going to be a group cuddle? **looks at the boys and smiles winningly** Because, we'll definitely need all the mouths to eat that many cupcakes. I love a good group cuddle. *shakes head* Sorry, back to the interview! So, I happen to know on good authority that you like chick flicks. I myself love chick flicks, but I have a soft spot for musicals and oldies. If you were to star in your own flick, would you be a Fred Astaire, a Cary Grant, a Clark Gable or Howard Keel?

Blake: Awesome choices, babe. I like the way Howard Keel showed how a big guy can be masculine, light on this feet and a real charmer. But that Cary Grant. He's a smooth ladies man, just like me.

Ayden: *Snorts laughter* You're as smooth as gravel.

Jen: *grins* I was hoping you'd say Fred Astaire, he's my love, past and present. It's the dancing, let's be honest. But I do love me some Howard Keen! *smiles at Blake*

Blake: Then why are Jen's beautiful eyes trained on me and not you?

Jen: *blinks* Ummm.... *Looks from Blake to Ayden to Matthias* FOOD! I happen to know you have some very earthy knowledge due to your "gifts". I want to know what spices and herbs you love and what you enjoy making with them?

Blake: I have many gifts I'd like to share with you, like—

Matthias: He's not allowed to cook anymore.

Blake: The fire wasn't *that* big. Besides, Mrs. Ishida said she wanted to remodel the kitchen anyways.

Ayden: Not the entire house too.

Jen: *giant eyes - mouth forms a soundless "O"*

Blake: *Shoots an irritated squint at Ayden* Tamarind seeds are my fave. I whip up some paste with them along with a few Habanero peppers for Jayden and he makes the most awesome BBQ sauce ever. He lets me cook the ribs.

Ayden: He lets you stand by the Bar-B-Q while he cooks the ribs.

Jen: I *love* BBQ!

Blake: I'm pretty sure this is *my* interview.

Jen: Now Blake, don't worry about them, *winks at Matthias* they're just being...brotherly.

Next question! Toward the end of the book you and the boys end up in a fairly hefty predicament and you end up keeping something very large from crumbling down. While I'm impressed with your muscular abilities, that's not why it's my favorite scene. It's my favorite scene of you because we get to see a side of you that seems a bit more real. For all the ladies sakes, including my own, could you let us in on another very real -and serious- thing about you?

Blake: I'm seriously in love with you.

Jen: Awwww. I think we need a group hug.

Ayden: Blake!

Blake: I'm *really* in love with her?

Matthias: *Stabs Blake with warning glare*

Jen: Matthias, it's really okay. *grins*

Blake: *Sighs. Squirms.* My parents left me because of the Mandatum.

Ayden: *Flinches. Squeezes Blake's shoulder.*

Blake: It hurts. But I have my uncle and...I understand. It's not that they don't love me or...you know...it's just....

Jen: *wipes away tear*

Matthias: Next question.

Jen: *give warning glare to Matthias* That's my line!

Blake: But the society did get me a new family! *Yanks Ayden and Matthias into hug*

Matthias: Ugh! Get off!

Jen: Hey! *jumps up* What about me? I want a hug!

Ayden: Let go! Ow! Matthias, that was me!

Jen: Fine. *hugs self* Next Question. Your personality never ceases to make me giggle and sigh. You may indeed be an endless flirt, but then again, so am I. I want you to use your very best pickup line on me and let's see if it works.

Blake: Finally we get to the good part.

Ayden: *Smirks and crosses arms* Oh, I can't wait to hear this.

Blake: *Leans forward and brushes Jen's hair off her shoulder*

Jen: *goosebumps race down neck*

Matthias: *Sits up frowning* What are you doing?

Blake: *Smiles. Glides fingers down Jen's neck to hook into the collar of Jen's shirt and checks tag.* Just checking if she was made in heaven.

Jen: *slumps down* *giggles*

Ayden: *Snorts* Seriously?

Jen: *laughs harder*

Blake: Yeah. I mean, she's almost perfect. The only thing that's wrong are her lips. They aren't on mine.

Jen: *dies laughing* Touché!

Matthias: **Gags** Jen, please change the subject.

Jen: But it's hilarious! I kinda love him for it. **grins**

Ayden: **Drops to knees** I will beg if you want me to.

Blake: Jeeze you guys are dramatic. The truth is, my best pick-up line is, "Tell me about yourself." Women fascinate me. And there's nothing sexier than really getting to know them.

Jen: **gazes at Blake** You know, Hun. **scoots a little closer to Blake** Those three sentences? Perfect.

Ayden and Matthias look at each other, confused

Matthias: Did he just say something…honest and…

Ayden: Intelligent and meaningful?

Matthias: Yeah.

Ayden: What was in Jen's cupcakes?

Jen: **blinks a couple times** Ummmm.... Next question! I'm not much of a flower person. That isn't to say I don't love flowers, but I'd rather plant them and watch them grow than have them purchased for me. This mostly stands because I'd rather have several books instead of the $40 bouquet of flowers. If you were going to plant a flower, particularly for me, what type of flower would it be and why? (Just so you know, I'm not a carnation fan and roses don't really impress me, I like different and sometimes I prefer exotic simplicity which could very well be an oxymoron)

Blake: The only thing that could come close to your beauty is the passiflora.

Ayden: Nice geek speak.

Blake: I'm going to ignore you because you have no game. *Reaches behind Jen and draws back to offer her a passiflora.* *It's unique and passionate, and bears the fruit of love. Just like you.

Jen: *eyes pop*

Ayden: You're reduced to magic tricks and I'm the one with no game?

Blake: The only thing magical here is the way Jen makes me feel.

Jen: Awwwww....I heart you Blake! *smiles and takes flower* Sometimes life is a bit much and I can't stand all the commotion and things going on around me, so I have a spot I like to go and chill out until I can deal. My closet. It's big, and full of books. Do you have a spot you like to go and find your own inner peace? Where?

Blake: When things go crazy, I go to Logan's house. Mrs. Hough usually has music playing and teaches me new dance moves. Mr. Hough and Logan let me help tear apart and rebuild cars in their garage. Logan has me do all the dirty work. But's that's alright, I like it dirty.

Jen: *snorts*

Ayden: I think she meant like a quiet place.

Matthias: It's emotionally quiet. And grounding.

Ayden and Blake: *Raise eyebrows at Matthias.*

Matthias: *Shifts uncomfortably* Would be my guess.

Jen: *gazes at Matthias* That's why I bake. *smiles and shakes head*

Okay! This or that?! Say the first thing that comes to your head. Hugs or Kisses?

Blake: Kisses!

Ayden: You really had to ask?

Jen: *grins*

Blake: I know you were thinking it too, babe. It's okay, you don't have to resist me.

Matthias: *Yanks Blake back.*

Jen: *air kisses* Milk or Lemonade?

Blake: Making out under the lemon tree.

Jen: *frowns* Not an option!

Matthias: You disgust me.

Jen: Brown or Blonde?

Blake: Brunettes. No contest. *Winks at Jen.*

Jen: *winks back* Handcuffs or Rope?

Blake: Rope. Wait. On me or you?

Ayden: Give it a rest.

Blake: Is that what you told Aurora when you whipped out the handcuffs?

Jen: *bedroom eyes at Ayden*

Ayden: Who am I to ruin your fun? Next question!

Jen: *waggles eyebrows* Jeans or Skirt?

Blake: Mini skirt! No. Tight jeans! You'll just have to try them both on so I can decide.

Jen: I don't do mini skirts, but I love me some jeans! However....Book or Movie?

Blake: Movies! You know, let's go see a Rom-Com right now. I'd never pass up the chance to go into a dark room with you, babe.

Jen: *sigh* *pets book cover*

Matthias: *Stands up.* Okay, let's go.

Ayden: Yep, you've officially crossed the line into creeper territory.

Jen: *Stands up* Wait!

Blake: Why are you always trying to ruin my relationships?

Ayden: What relationships?

Blake: Jen and I have been going steady for at least ten minutes now.

Jen: *snorts*

Ayden: And we've gone from creepy to delusional.

Matthias: *Drags Blake away.*

Jen: Wait! You didn't give me a goodbye hug! *sniffles*

Blake: *Shakes off Matthias* Babe! Tell them about our deep connection!

Matthias: *Opens door*Ayden, it's that time.

Blake: Don't let our love be doomed like Romeo and Cleopatra!

Jen: *dies laughing*

Ayden: *Runs and tackles Blake through door*

Matthias: So sorry he wasted your time. Have a lovely day, Jen. *Shuts door* Ayden, you can't set him on fire. Blake, just get in the car

Jen: *stares at door* Ummm.... *puzzled look* Bye? I'll miss you? Thanks for the hugs all around? *sigh*

I must say that I'm still rather depressed about the lack of hugs for myself, but then again, they all did the interview shirtless, so I was okay. I hope you guys all enjoyed meeting the Hex Boys! I loved interviewing them and can't wait for my cuddle with Blake! (Melissa, he's older in my head! Missie, you can't deny they want me! Jenny, I'll Twitter smite you any day, booya!! Felicia, sorry that I suck at sharing men, even if there are 6. Tina...have you finished yet? Ladies, on a positive note, they are indeed willing to move all of our stuff shirtless!)

THE HEX BOYS

Host: Heidi at Rainy Day Ramblings

Question: "What is the best thing about dating each one of you?"

Blake: Oh wow. There are so many good things about dating me I don't even know where to begin.

Matthias: Then don't.

Blake: I'm beyond handsome. And look at these muscles! *Flexes massive arms* I can sweep a dozen girls off their feet with—

Ayden: You're forgetting the worst thing about dating you.

Blake: What's that?

Tristan: They're dating you.

Blake: Dude, that's so a pro. You're just jealous because when I kiss a girl, she feels the earth move.

Ayden: You can use your tricks, but let's not forget you failed the Seduction Course.

Blake: I didn't fail. I was kicked out.

Logan: Yeah, because that's so much better.

Ayden: One of the best things about dating me is that I not only passed the Seduction Course, I was top of my class.

Tristan: But you might light a girl on fire.

Jayden: As I understand it, most females look for a mate who will light their fire.

Blake: But not all of them would like Ayden's handcuffs.

Ayden: Shut up! That was a one time only—

Tristan: You're making it sound worse.

Logan: *Points at Blake* If you say anything about me, you're—

Blake: Logan's a great dancer. And we all know a guy who can dance, is good in—

Logan: *Puts hands over ears* La, la, la, la, la!

Jayden: I don't know why you're embarrassed. Sexual attraction is a key component to—

Tristan: Ugh! Please stop talking.

Jayden: But that's my most attractive quality. I'm happy to communicate.

Ayden: But half the time, no one knows what you're saying. Including me, and I'm your brother.

Jayden: Since women are innately circumlocutory, I believe in this instance, you derogate their appreciation of my loquacious propensities.

Ayden: *Sighs* You just proved my point.

Blake: And Jayden will be totally oblivious to her romantic advances. Unlike me.

Ayden: Who imagines them.

Blake: Hey! That's not—

Tristan: Yes, it is. The only thing bigger than your ego is your delusion that you're some sort of irresistible—

Blake: And what's so great about dating you? A computer geek who never takes a risk on anything.

Tristan: That's not true. I'd risk everything for the right girl.

Blake: And leave all the other girls as demon bait? Dude, that's cold. I, on the other hand, risk everything for every girl.

Tristan: That's not what I meant! Quit twisting—

Matthias: Start bickering like school girls again and I'll make sure you're all demon bait.

Tristan: Fine, Matthias. Let's talk about your fine dating qualities. Does dark and brooding count?

Matthias: *Glares* We can leave me out of this, mate.

Logan: He's...uh...loyal?

Jayden: And extremely well-read. Especially in regard to classical ro—

Matthias: That's enough.

Blake: He's got whips.

Matthias: Shut it, you idiot! *Grabs Blake in headlock*

Blake: Anger management issues!

Ayden: When it comes to you, we all have anger management issues.

Blake: *Fails to break Matthias' grip* Guys! *Wheezes* Little help?

Ayden: I think we'd better end this before he makes us sound like kinky, hormonal maniacs.

Logan: Too late.

TRISTAN

Host: Faye at Ramblings of a Teenage Bookworm

Faye: Thanks so much for joining me today Tristan!

Tristan: Thanks for having me.

Faye: Since you aren't a central character, why don't you tell my readers a little about yourself first?

Tristan: Uh. Okay. I, um, I'm the tech expert. For our demon hunting team. I also make sure we stay on track. Don't do anything stupid. Or too dangerous. They say I'm the worry-wart but somebody has to keep these guys in line. They can all be such hot heads. Acting before they think things through. Although Jayden usually thinks too much. The six of us are practically always together. Which is annoying sometimes. Most of the time. But it's safer to have a buddy system than privacy. Unless your buddy is Blake. You're better off alone if there's a girl in his sights.

Door bangs open. Gasps all around.

Blake: Behold! The girl of my dreams!

Tristan: Are you kidding?! I snuck out my window to avoid you following me!

Blake: *Kneels before Faye and takes her hand* I've been waiting for you my whole life.

Tristan: *Shoves Blake away from Faye* I even switched off the tracker in my car! Made sure I didn't have a tail!

Jayden: *Enters with look of relief* Ah, Tristan. Excellent! You're unharmed. Blake saw you abscond out your window and feared you were in some sort of danger. His qualms became mine when I ascertained your car tracker was inoperative. Fortunately, I was able to activate it remotely.

Tristan: *Sighs* Thanks Jayden. *Turns to Blake* I even told you my interviewer was an old man.

Blake: *Throws arm around Faye* How dare you insult her so! It's alright babe, I think you're gorgeous!

Jayden: You say that about every female we encounter.

Blake: You're a terrible wing man.

Jayden: I don't have a pilot's license.

Faye: So you're a Hex Boy, right?

Tristan: One of the group, but yeah.

Faye: What does that mean exactly?

Blake: It means we have hex appeal.

Tristan: *Laughs* It's something the kids at school started calling us. After we became demon hunters we kept to ourselves…distanced ourselves from the normal kids—

Jayden: I warned you all that separating ourselves would bring unwanted attention.

Tristan: Yes, but we agreed that the community would be safer. We became the odd balls. And trouble seemed to follow us so we were "hexed," I think was the general consensus.

Jayden: Additionally, hex is derives from Greek meaning six and there are six of us.

Blake: The six dangerously, sexy guys of Gossamer Falls. I'm the bad boy of the group. If you're into that. Otherwise I'm not—

Tristan: Important. Next question?

Faye: How do you guys pull off going to High School and being Demon Hunters? It seems kind of complicated if you ask me lol.

Tristan: It's just like having a part-time job while going to school. And depending on how strong the demon is, sometime it only takes two or three of us to take one down. So the rest of us can stay in class or at home and finish homework. The team effort makes it work.

Jayden: Tristan's abilities make the situation infinitely more facile.

Blake: No, Tristan makes it way easier.

Jayden: That what I just— *Throws up his hands*

Blake: We can skip out of class anytime or he convinces the teachers to give us A's.

Tristan: *Laughs nervously* I don't do that.

Jayden: You might consider at least giving him a B. Even with my tutoring he's failing English.

Blake: Because I have no idea what you're saying.

Jayden: Clearly.

Tristan: No, he should just read the book.

Jayden: He does. But inexplicably comes to utterly obtuse conclusions. Much like Aurora.

Blake: How can anyone believe that the Bennett chick thinks Heathcliff—

Tristan: Completely different books! *Turns to Jayden* Maybe a C.

Jayden: That would help.

Faye: What was your favorite part or scene of the D@D?

Tristan: You mean Operation DDHK? I don't have a favorite part. All of it was horrible! Demons kept trying to kill Aurora, my friends, me, then they used Herman—like we haven't ruined his life enough. I tried to help and ended up torturing Aurora—

Blake: Whoa, dude. Calm down that wasn't your fault.

Jayden: Well, technically—

Blake: *Grabs Jayden in headlock* What's that, logic boy? Yeah, Faye is more radiant than the sun.

Jayden: *Wrestles free* That makes no sense. Faye isn't luminescent in the slightest.

Faye: What do you see yourself doing in the say, next 10 years?

Blake: What do you see yourself doing? Because we could be doing it together.

Tristan: Unless she's smart and gets the restraining order. Let's see…in ten years—

Jayden: Of course such conjecture is predicated on the postulation that you're still alive.

Tristan: *Pales* You think I'm going to be dead?

Jayden: I'm simply verbalizing the possibility based on the Mandatum's mortality rate being much higher than those in the most hazardous professions of fishing or logging. And if you continue—

Tristan: Okay, let's assume I'm alive, I see myself semi-retired from actual hunting and working within the Mandatum's tech operations. I love computers and gadgets and they have the best. A lot of hunters with my abilities go into psychological operations but messing with people's heads is dangerous. And it'll get me drafted into the Sicarius. *shivers* Although I've got to find out how and why I affect Aurora like I do.

Faye: Overall, how do you think Alyssa and Eileen handled your story? I need me some more Hexy Boys!

Blake: Trust me, Babe, I'm the only Hexy Boy you need and you can have as much of me as you want.

Tristan: *Rolls eyes, pulls out phone to send quick text* Personally, I could do with one less. Seriously, Faye, I'll back you up on that restraining order. Anyway, about our story, Jayden, I thought you were writing it.

Jayden: I'm chronicling our experiences, yes.

Tristan: So are Alyssa and Eileen your ghost writers?

Jayden: I don't even know any ghosts. And if I did, I'd never entrust them with our story. Ghosts are notorious for affiliating with demons. And how would they type or write? Their ethereal embodiment would render that impossible.

Blake: *Waggles eyebrows* Faye's yum-body is meant for me. See what I did there?

Tristan: Shut up. The one problem with the story is that Aurora gets to tell her side, and sometimes it makes me look like a bad guy. Which I'm not. I know we made things worse, put her in danger, but remember, I tried to keep her out of this whole mess.

Jayden: Faye did suggest a spin-off. Then we could tell our version of events.

Blake: I'd need my own book. We could add a centerfold of me.

Tristan: I'm gonna be sick.

Faye: So things have gotten pretty exciting/crazy towards the end of D@D, what's next?

Tristan: We definitely need some questions answered in order to keep Aurora safe. Until we know more, we can't trust anyone. And I have a feeling Aurora isn't telling us everything.

Jayden: That's true. She often exudes a taciturn sense of reticence.

Blake: You think so? I always liked her perfume. But, Faye, let's get back to what's next for you and me. First, we should—

Door bursts open

Ayden: You going quietly this time Blake? *Rolls neck from side to side with audible pops*

Blake: *Gapes at Tristan* I can't believe you called Ayden!

Matthias: He didn't. He called me. I can't believe you didn't turn off the tracker in your car.

Tristan: I did! Jayden turned it back on!

Jayden: Why is everyone irate?

Blake: Don't worry babe, I won't let them take you.

Ayden: I'm not taking Faye. I'm taking you. She doesn't deserve your slobbering hormones. Time to leave her alone.

Blake: Never. We're meant to be!

Ayden: *Rolls eyes* If I had a nickel.

Matthias: He never makes it easy, does he? *Black whip snaps out and wraps around Blake and Matthias drags him outside*

Ayden: *Smiles at Faye* Since Blake's gone, I'd be happy to stay and chat.

Matthias: *Yells from outside* I heard that! You're not leaving me alone with this moron. I'll drag you all out if I have to. But, uh, not you, Faye.

Ayden: *Shrugs* Was worth a try.

Tristan: *Pushing Jayden out the door* Thanks. And keep in mind, that restraining order is always an option.

THE HEX BOYS

Host: The Kirks at Teens Read and Write

Question: "What would you do on Valentine's Day?"

Ayden: I'd borrow the family jet and take her to Paris.

Blake: Bring me back some ribs!

Ayden: Not Texas! Paris, France. We'd get there early so I could take her on a shopping spree on the Faubourg Saint-Honoré which houses designers like Versace, Hermes, Chanel, Christian Doir, and Yves Saint Laurent. She'd get all decked out in some of her new clothes and we'd take a luxurious boat ride on the Seine River. Afterwards we'd head up to the top of the Eiffle Tower and enjoy a romantic dinner at Le Jules Verne. We'd stay up all night exploring the City of Lights, have a delicious breakfast in a quaint cafe then hit the best chocolatiers in town to stock up for the ride home.

Blake: Paris? Psh, lame. I'd take my babe on horseback through the mountains up to the falls. Then we'd have a picnic on top of the waterfalls. She'll be so overwhelmed by my romantic side that she'll swoon into my arms and-

Ayden: Die because she ate something you made.

Blake: I'd never jeopardize my lady like that! I'd have Jayden make the picnic. He's my wing man.

Jayden: I'd cook for my Valentine as well after I took her to-

Ayden: You can't take her to a lab or conduct experiments on her.

Jayden: Who is to say my potential mate wouldn't like laboratories?

Ayden: Me. Not on V-day she doesn't. She wants romantic.

Jayden: A liaison of sorts. Hm...I'd commandeer the family yacht and set sail to a remote location where we could surf together. I'd ensure there'd be perfect waves. Look at me being whimsical!

Tristan: I'd keep my date low key. Buy out the theatre for the day and have them play all my Valentine's favorite movies. Space Odyessy, Ghost Busters, The Matrix.

Blake: Her favorites or yours?

Tristan: Hers. What girl doesn't like Star Wars?

Blake: Trust me, dude, stick to Rom-Coms.

Logan: We'd have dinner at the country club. And I'd have professional dancers come and reenact my Valentine's favorite dance number from her favorite musical. Then I'd dance her over so she could star in it.

Ayden: Are you going to dance too?

Logan: Of course. I wouldn't throw her up there and watch, I'd lead her through it.

Ayden: Tristan!

Tristan: Don't worry, I've already got the camera.

Matthias: *Crickets chirp in the silence*

Tristan: Come on, just answer the question.

Jayden: It's hypothetical.

Ayden: Especially since no girl is brave enough to get within a hundred yards of you.

Logan: *Mutters* Or insane enough.

Blake: Told you to work on your chivalry.

Matthias: *Sighs* England. I'd take my Valentine to England on a tour of the places from Jane Austen's books. Derbyshire, Mr. Darcy's house. Places like that.

Ayden: You're really milking that dark, brooding thing.

AYDEN

Host: Jenny at Supernatural Snark

Today I have a very special interview with a certain Hex Boy who may or may not be completely and utterly in love with me. It happens a lot. I'm very lovable you see. Anyway, I've invited Ayden here for a little chat so we can discuss our love out in the open and share it with the world. Don't be jealous everyone, sure Ayden is mine (and Blake too) but there's a fictional someone out there for all of you as well!

In all seriousness though, I've had an absolute blast on the promotional tour for Demons at Deadnight and I'm beyond thrilled to share some of the witty banter A&E Kirk do so well in this story with all of you. I hope the interview makes you laugh as much as it did me and Happy Friday!

Jenny: What's the very first thing that ran through your mind when Aurora fell and managed to land astride you? I would just like to remind you that I am the epitome of a mature individual and my mind absolutely NEVER dips into the gutter, so let's keep this answer clean ;-)

Ayden: *Grins.* First of all, I've seen your tweets, so I'm not buying the innocent act. But I'll do my best. I noticed her sweaty t-shirt clinging in all the right places and yoga pants that followed every curve of those endless legs. I'm a guy. I felt some heat. And in my case that can be dangerous, which is why I did what I did. To protect her. Although, I've been working on my control. So why don't you and I reenact the scenario and see how I handle it now?

Don't believe him dear readers! I am a paragon of innocence and virtue. And class. A PARAGON I TELL YOU! Ayden, stop trying to corrupt me with your many charms. I'm immune. And I'll meet you for that reenactment anytime and anyplace ;-)

Jenny: If you could trade abilities with one of the other Hex Boys for a day, whom would you most like to switch with and what would you do with the new ability first?

Ayden: Don't ever tell him this, but I'd switch with Blake. It'd be nice to actually bring life into the world, instead of turning everything ash. I'd recreate the gardens of Versailles. Then we could take a walk and—

Jayden: I don't know why you're embarrassed. That cerebral thread has logical merit.

Ayden: *sighs*

Jayden: I'm sure you're befuddled trying to aggregate my reasons for being here.

Ayden: I gave up years ago trying to understand a brother like you.

Jayden: Blake was inquiring as to your interview venue. This is embarrassing to admit, but as inept as Blake is, he always seems to get the better of me. So I thought it best to leave the premises before I unwittingly unveiled your location.

Ayden: By coming to my location?

Jayden: You don't give me enough credit. My stealth techniques—

Blake: Suck!

Jayden: *Hangs head* I'm never going to live this down.

Blake: Yes, you'll never live this down Logic Boy because I so owned you! Jenny, a highly intelligent and gorgeous babe like you finds brains attractive. This is my way of proving that I'm worthy of your love.

Ayden: If you touch her, you'll never be able to use your hands again.

Blake: What if she touches me?

Jenny reaches for both Ayden and Blake here. Two hands. Two boys. Perfect mathematical outcome

Ayden: Keep dreaming.

Jenny: Can you share with us any funny stories from when you, the boys, and Aurora were kids?

Blake: How about we go somewhere quiet and write our own romance, Jenny.

Blake! Just how easy do you think I am? Please scroll up to question one and take note of the paragon of innocence exclamation. With that clearly stated for all to read I'd just like to say I'm really digging historical romances at the moment, so maybe we can romance ourselves in that general direction. Also, romance novel heroes almost NEVER wear shirts. Ever. They're perpetually shirtless. Let's start there...

Jayden: Back then Blake employed the ridiculous notion that girls possessed cooties.

Ayden: I miss those days.

Blake: That's before I met babes like Jenny.

Ayden: Well, the first time we met Aurora, she beat Jayden over the head with her picture book.

Jayden: I was simply trying to point out its inaccuracy regarding the fanciful personification of animals.

Blake: I'd have hit you too.

Jenny: Let's talk romance for a second (you can thank me later for bringing this topic up – kisses are an acceptable form of payment. Just saying.). On a date with a girl, who is most likely to wind up getting slapped? Most likely to land a first date kiss? Most likely to come up with the strangest activity to do on a date?

Blake: Romance? Kisses as payment? Will you keep me?

Ayden: Keep you locked up in her basement so that she can have what she really wants. Me.

Blake: *Snorts* Please.

Jayden: Gentlemen, you digress.

Ayden: Sorry, Jenny. Most likely to get slapped is Jayden.

Jayden: Me?! What about Blake?

Blake: You're the only one who brings up fallopian tubes.

Jenny falls out of her chair laughing. Snorting may also be involved

Ayden: Logan's shy charm, almost as irresistible as mine, would land the kiss.

Blake: It'd be a waste because he'd faint.

Ayden: And Matthias would come up with the strangest activity.

Blake: Not Jayden?

Jayden: Hey!

Ayden: No way. Can you imagine Matthias with a girl?

Blake: He'd probably sacrifice her on an altar so some god would get rid of Aurora.

Jayden: Or they'd do needlepoint.

Ayden: Exactly. And as for me, I'd be the one most likely to get a second date. And a—

Blake: You're the one most likely to make me throw up.

Jenny: If I were to make a pass at you, hypothetically speaking of course, what would you say my chances of successfully landing a date with you would be? I'm asking for strictly professional interview purposes only. Obviously. (If my chances aren't so good, can we maybe direct this question to the other boys as well? Thanks.)

Ayden: The jet's fueled. How about dinner in Paris?

Blake: Yuck. Who wants stinky frog legs? Pick me! I'll give you a ride you won't forget.

Who says I'd let you be the one doing the riding? I'll show you how to get ridden...

Ayden and Jayden: Blake!

Blake: A horseback ride. Jeez, you guys have dirty minds.

Oops. I went in the gutter too. My bad. I thought that was where we were all headed. No? Just me and Ayden and Jayden then?

Jenny: You're a little smug and a little self-satisfied when it comes to Aurora's physical reactions to you (and damn if isn't irritatingly attractive). What is the best line you've either used on a girl or heard used on a girl to make a memorable first impression?

Ayden: I don't like to use lines because they seem dishonest and I like to better spend my time asking questions and getting to know the real person. But I have to admit, after meeting you, falling asleep is useless because the reality of you is far better than any dream.

Blake: Oh, come on, dude. That was so a line! A good one—and I'll use it— but so a line!

Ayden: Are you saying I'm wrong?

Blake: Of course not. Jenny's awesome but… *sighs* I hate you.

Ayden: You're the one who got kicked out of the seduction course.

Blake: I knew everyone called it that!

Jenny: Okay, I'll ease up on the romantic stuff for now.

Blake: What? No! Romance is where I shine!

Ayden: Obviously not if she's changing subject.

Jenny: If for some reason your abilities with fire were to go on the fritz, what other type of weapon would you feel most comfortable battling demonic forces with?

Ayden: An iron chain whip, fringed with blades. It's got weight, fluidity and ultimate damage capability.

Blake: Hey, Jenny, if you like whips, I like whips. And I know a guy…

I have to say I enjoy how this conversation keeps making its way back to the gutter. It wouldn't be a Friday here without some sexual innuendo and inappropriate comments. I'm a little in love with you right now Blake, not gonna lie

Jenny: Your parents are fans of expressing their gratitude to others with hugely extravagant gifts. What, big or small, is the best gift you think they've ever given you?

Ayden: *Shakes head* Other people get the extravagant stuff. Not us. I'm just happy we're still all together.

Blake: That's the ultimate gift, dude. *Blake breathes deep* But those sports cars are sweet.

Jayden: We only received them after they were damaged during overseas transit and destined for the junkyard.

Ayden: *Laughs* One even had to be fished out of the harbor. We worked in Logan's dad auto shop to pay for parts while he and Logan helped us put the cars back together. It took months.

Jayden: They did give us the game room.

Ayden: True. Although, some might argue they only gave it to us because somebody set our kitchen on fire.

Blake: I told you that was an accident!

Jenny: Have you ever inadvertently lit something of vital importance on fire?

Ayden: Jayden's homework.

Jayden: That was on purpose.

Ayden: So you keep saying.

Blake: As long as you don't light Jenny on fire because she's vitally important to me.

Flattery will get you everywhere with me. Let's go back to that question about riding...

Ayden: Don't worry. I don't light her on fire. I just light her fire.

You sweet talker you! What else can you do with your mouth?

Jayden: Is that a line? Why are you using it on Blake?

Jenny: Which would you rather face: a pissed off demon, a pissed off Guardian, or a pissed off Aurora?

Ayden: Demon. I have a lot more experience with them. And much more chance of survival.

Door bangs open.

Matthias: What about a pissed off Matthias?

Jayden: **Shrugs** We deal with that every day.

Logan and Tristan: **Push past Matthias** We have to get out of here.

Ayden: My session isn't over yet.

Matthias: That's because it's not a session. It's an interview. **Lights flicker.** With a civilian.

Ayden: **Looks confused at Jenny** You're not a shrink?

Um. Not technically. But if that's what does it for you Ayden, consider me shrinky in every possible way

Matthias: None of them have been.

Jayden: Of course not. Why would you think that?

Matthias: Because you told us you'd received orders from the Mandatum that our team had to have mandatory interviews with psychologists!

Jayden: I didn't say that.

All the other Hex Boys: Yes you did!

Jayden: No, I said—

Matthias: Ayden, you're supposed to translate him! How could you miss this?

Ayden: Since when is that my job?

Matthias: Tristan, take care of Jenny.

Blake: **Hugs Jenny to shield her** Wait! I don't want her to forget how much she loves me!

Tristan: What if she's like Aurora? I don't want to hurt—

Matthias: Are you two kidding me right now?! Logan!

Logan: **Jumps on Blake's back and gets him in headlock.**

Blake: Get off! **Spins wildly. Yanks on Logan's tie.** I love her!

Tristan: Logan, ease up. He might pass out!

Logan: **Grunts** That's the plan.

Jayden: Your manic behavior is unnecessary. Everyone thinks our experiences are fictional.

All Hex Boys freeze

Matthias: Explain.

Jayden: These exceptional ladies who we've been talking to are highly respected book bloggers. Since I'm chronicling our adventures, I was curious to study the real world's response to our paranormal one. So I set up these interviews to receive feedback.

Ayden: *Groans* It's one of his experiments.

Matthias: *Squints* And they think this is all make believe.

Blake: *Panicked* But our love is real!

Blake!!!!! OUR LOVE IS SO REAL! IT'S THE REAL-EST! It cannot be contained. Or doused. It is ever-growing and all-encompassing. In fact, I think my love can grow large enough to include all 6 of you. We'll be a love hexagon! A LOVE HEXAGON BOYS! Think about it. It's never been done. We'll be blazing a trail. A love trail! A trail o'love!

Jayden: As if we're literary characters. Logan shy but strong. Tristan concerned and overprotective. Blake larger than life.

Blake: So true.

Jayden: And comic relief

Blake: Hey!

Jayden: Me, the genius.

Blake: And weird.

Jayden: Ayden the smoldering, sexy hottie.

Blake: Oh, sure, give him the good part.

Ayden: Art imitating life.

Tristan: Did he just say "hottie"?

Logan: *Climbing off Blake* It's literary speak.

Jayden: *To Matthias* And you're—

Matthias: *Shakes head* The dark, brooding one with the tortured past. Bugger. *Mutters under breath* Wouldn't mum love that. *Smiles. Dimples show.* Books. This is all about books. *Takes Jenny's hand and bows* Miss Jenny, you just made my day. Thank you. *Turns to Hex Boys* Mates, take all the time you need.

Whuh. Was it my talk of the love hexagon that won him over? My claims of virtue maybe? Matthias! Don't go! We can start building the hexagon right now!

Hex Boys stare as Matthias leaves

Tristan: What just happened?

Logan: The world just turned upside down.

Jayden: Matthias may need medical attention.

Ayden: *Nods* We'd better follow him.

Blake: I'm getting my group hug! *Tries to gather everyone together*

Ayden: Blake, get your hand off my—

Blake: Whoops! Thought that was—

Ayden: We're outta here. And Jenny, let me know when you're up for Paris.

Jayden: She thinks you're fictitious.

Ayden: Which is why our time together will be…*winks at Jenny*…unreal.

Blake: *Being dragged out the door* Dude, that is so a line! Ignore him, Jenny. I'll be back when I'm eighteen!

Jenny dies of all the hotness

MATTHIAS

Host: Melissa, Books and Things

Those of you just joining us and missed the last interview, should see me try to interview one of the most mysterious Hex boy in the group. While some people may be turned off by his brash behavior, others will wonder if he isn't hiding huge depths to his personality. I'll try to get to the bottom of that with my interview.

Melissa: I'm so glad to meet again! We were interrupted the last time we tried to talk. Finally, a moment to get to know you.

Matthias: Thanks, Melissa. You're very kind. I apologize for the last time. It's those idiots that I can never seem to ditch completely, but today, I think I have it handled. Ask away.

Melissa: For those that have not met you in the first book, what can you tell us about yourself and your brothers?

Matthias: We're not supposed to talk about this so I'll just say I'm in charge of our team of six guys who have special powers which we use to fight demons. I'm from Australia and moved to Gossamer Falls about eight years ago with my Dad who's the sheriff. The rest of the guys already lived there, and we've been together as a team ever since. Technically they aren't my brothers. We've just been through a lot together. We're...close. As for my power, let's just say I have a dark side.

Melissa: Can you tell us anything about the Mandatum?

Matthias: Not much. The Mandatum is an ancient secret society that covers the globe and is made up of those dedicated to destroying evil. But you can't go around talking about this, Melissa, otherwise we'll have to send Tristan to take care of your memory to keep you safe. The Mandatum takes it secret status seriously.

Blake bursts through the door

Blake: Just make sure she doesn't forget me! Not that anyone ever could.

Matthias: I wish I could. What are you doing here? Never mind. Go away.

Blake: Melissa begged me to come. Or she would have if someone had let me talk to her. She's my soul mate. Or she would be if we ever got to spend time together. But don't worry. I'll be quiet. I'm just here to bask in the beauty that is Melissa. *Takes Melissa's hand and stares lovingly into her eyes*

Melissa: Between all of you, you have a lot of supernatural abilities so I have to ask, what is your biggest inner strength?

Blake: His biggest inner strength would probably be his heart. Killer resting heart rate. Although we're all in great shape. Or maybe it's his abs. Not as awesome as mine of course. Wanna see? *starts to lift shirt*

Matthias: *yanks shirt down* You idiot! She's talking about emotional inner strength.

Blake: Oh. *shoves off Matthias then flashes shirt up and down quickly before Matthias can stop him* See? Wanna jump me now?

Matthias: No she does not! But I want to thump you now.

Blake: I'm flattered, dude, but you're not my type. Melissa, did I mention I was twenty-one now?

Matthias: You haven't even turned eighteen!

Blake: I'm inner emotionally twenty-one.

Matthias: Your inner emotion is negative two.

Blake: Well, you're worse. Your inner emotion is zero.

Matthias: *frowns* Zero would actually be higher than— Never mind. Melissa, my inner strength would be the ability to stay calm and remain focused in dire situations when everyone else panics. These morons let their emotions take over. Or in Blake's case, his hormones.

Blake: Melissa can take over my hormones any day. *winks at Melissa*

Melissa: What about your weakness for kids?

Matthias: *Shifts uncomfortably** Kids are innocent. Need to be protected. They should never have to deal with evil or pain. No one, especially me, should ever show them anything but kindness.

Blake: *Claps Matthias on the shoulder and smiles at Melissa** Hey beautiful babe, how about your next awesome question?

Melissa: Are you dating anyone? What kind of girl would you like? How do you feel about Aurora and Ayden? Any juicy gossip about the others? ;)

Matthias: *lights flicker as he clenches jaw** Dating? Who told you? Is this about that newspaper article? Stupid Aurora set me up. I am not "looking for love."

Blake: So you are dating someone?

Matthias: I never said that.

Blake: You never didn't not say that.

Matthias: If I was dating someone, I wouldn't kiss and tell so—

Blake: Why would you have to tell her? If you kissed her, wouldn't she know? Or do you kiss so badly she wouldn't be able to tell?

Matthias: I kiss just fine.

Blake: Says who?

Matthias: Says no one!

Blake: Then how do you know? Maybe Melissa would volunteer to judge your kissing skills. Take her in your arms and pucker up. I'll be an impractical observer.

Matthias: Shut up!

Blake: What? It's for science.

Matthias: Sorry, Melissa. Okay, as for a girl, strong and independent.

Blake: Like Aurora?

Matthias: No! *shoves Blake away* She'd have to enjoy books, have a good sense of humor.

Blake: To make up for your lack of one.

Matthias: I put up with you, don't I? She'd need to be able to keep secrets, understand the whole Mandatum thing. Love kids and family. Enjoy spending time together just her and me. I'm not a big crowd kind of guy.

Blake: This dream girl is sounding a lot like Aurora.

Matthias: No she isn't. In fact, let's say that my dream girl is everything opposite of Aurora. Period.

Blake: My dream girl is everything Melissa.

Matthias: *rolls eyes* As for Aurora and Ayden, he took this whole pretend boyfriend thing way too far. I knew it would be a disaster. I'm just hoping he gets it out of his system soon, before she gets him killed. She's already proven she's dangerous for him. For all of us. And I don't have any gossip because I can keep a secret, unlike blabbermouth Blake.

Blake: Hurtful, dude.

Melissa: Favorite books? Favorite music? Favorite anything else?

Blake: He has tons of books, especially those old weird talking ones.

Matthias: He means the classics. I was raised on Shakespeare, Greek Epics, Edgar Allan Poe, Mark Twain. I go for classical music as well. It was always playing at our house. It reminds me of...better times.

Blake: Elevator music? Yuck!

Matthias: That's not the same music at all! I can't talk to you. Favorite food would be Mrs. Lahey's banana bread or my dad's key lime pie. Favorite pastime is annoying Aurora until I can figure out how to get her out of our lives.

Blake: But she's part of the team now so—

Matthias: And I also have to figure out how convince the rest of the idiots she's not part of the team.

Blake: She's so part of the team and dude, I am so your brother. Aurora's like your big sister. We're family! Which means since Melissa is my one and only, she's your girlfriend-in-law! Which means maybe the whole kissing her thing wasn't such a good idea. We'll find you someone else to practice on.

Matthias: This is a nightmare. We're outta here. Thanks Melissa. Always a pleasure. *takes Melissa's hand and kisses it*

Blake: You're outta here. Melissa and I are just getting started. And what did I just tell you about kissing my girlfriend? Although, I guess she could score you on it. You know, with a paddle, like on that dancing show. *mouth breaks into a sly* *grin** And then Melissa and I could use the paddle later to get all kinds of kink—

*black whip materializes and wraps around Blake**

Blake: No! Oh...wait a minute. I get it. Whips! Good idea Matthias. Although you should see how well you score first and then ask Melissa if she's into the whole group—

*Matthias yanks Blake out the door**

Blake: *calls from outside** Melissa! Find me my love! Ow! That hurt. Dude, we really need a safe word.

THE HEX BOYS

Host: Natalie

Hi guys. Welcome to my stop on The Divinicus Nex Chronicles by A&E Kirk. I'm so so excited to be on this tour because I adored book 1, ever since I read it when it came out it's been firmly on my favourites shelf and it's one of my all-time favourite books EVER (plus just look at those covers)!! I have book 2 to read after my current read and I can't wait!!! Seriously guys, this is a series that needs to be read, you need to be introduced to the HEX BOYS!!! Anyway, check out the AMAZING guest post I have for you today from the Hex Boys, they are discussing their favorite things, enter the awesome giveaway and then continue on the tour. So without further ado, I present you with

Blake: Hellooo Natalie! We are stoked to be here! And hello to all the other lovely ladies out there! We have come to make your day because you deserve only the best, and that's us! Well, mostly me, but the guys tagged along so you have to at least act like you're interested in what they have to say. Careful guys, she's Irish. She might blast you with her fiery temper. Not me though. She loves me.

Logan: *rolls eyes* Natalie does want us all here. She's been one of our biggest supporters for a long time. She's asked us here to talk about our favorite things, not for you to flirt.

Blake: I can't help it. Flirting is in my CPA.

Logan: It's DNA.

Blake: That too.

Logan: I give up.

Blake: I never give up on the ladies. Especially you, Natalie. *winks* And Logan, that's the difference between you and me. It's why you don't have a girlfriend.

Tristan: That's the only reason? I thought it was because he practically faints anytime a girl smiles at him.

Logan: *Blushes* I do not. And you don't have girlfriend either, Blake.

Blake: Only because I can't decide on one. I don't have the heart to disappoint the lesions of Team Blake's adoring fans.

Jayden: You mean legions. Fans wouldn't be a type of injury.

Logan: They would if they were Blake's fans.

Tristan: He doesn't have any fans!

Blake: You're just mad because you don't even have a team.

Tristan: I could have a team.

Ayden: Hey, I'm impressed he knew the word "legumes." Give him some points for that.

Matthias: *growls* You bloody idiots! Just shut it and talk about your favorite things. Natalie doesn't want to hear your ridiculous babble, and we've got to get back to little things like ridding the world of demons.

Tristan: And keeping Aurora safe.

Matthias: That one can wait.

Ayden: *shoves Matthias's shoulder* You're such a jerk.

Matthias: Don't start with me. You're the one stupid enough to want to do the whole fake boyfriend fiasco so—

Tristan: Okay, but I can answer for Blake too. His favorite thing is girls.

Blake: You are so wrong. It's not girls. It's the ladies. And it's only because I'm their favorite thing so it's only fair. Quid pro quo and all.

Several beats of silence

Tristan: Did he just—

Ayden: Use quid pro quo—

Logan: Correctly in a sentence?

Jayden: I'm dumfounded.

Blake: Dude, you're one of the smartest guys I know. Don't call yourself dumb.

Ayden: And he's back.

Logan: *lets out long breath* Whew.

Tristan: Yeah, I feel better too.

Matthias: Come on! Sorry Natalie. Getting off track here. Back to favorite things. Blake's are gir— sorry, the ladies and—

Blake: Don't forget the great outdoors. Plants, trees, flowers blooming, mountains, deserts. I love everything about the earth. My favorite thing is exploring it and all its beauty. And I want to share it with all the—

Matthias: Ladies. We've got it. Logan?

Logan: Um, okay. My favorite things are cars. And driving them. Fast.

Blake: So, Logan likes fast cars and fast women.

Logan: *whacks Blake's shoulder* I didn't say fast women.

Blake: So you like slow women?

Matthias: Moving on. Jayden? And don't say science. Or big words.

Jayden: Are you expressing the desire that I don't verbalize large words or I can't express that they are my favorite thing? And by big, are you defining the actual length of the word or its level of complexity?

Matthias: *glares*

Jayden: Understood. While I do love cooking, I will denote my favorite thing as learning something new. Since my accumulation of knowledge is so immense, perceiving something of which I was previously unaware of circulates a tremendous joy. Which is why Aurora's anomalous propensities are so fascinating.

Matthias: The only thing fascinating is that you find Aurora fascinating. Tristan?

Tristan: It's Comic Con. Hands down.

Blake: Who's she? And why does she have her hands down? Is that some sort of kinky thing you two do?

Tristan: It's not a she, it's a convention. It's my favorite because it takes all of my favorite stuff, comic books, sci fi, fantasy, super heroes, video games, anime, and puts it under one roof. It's awesome! I go every year. I'm hoping to take my dad next time. He'd love it.

Ayden: It's nerdvana. Just like your bedroom.

Blake: I wanna go. She sounds fun. And kinky.

Tristan: It's not a girl!

Logan: Why didn't you ever take us?

Matthias: I wouldn't take us. Ayden, how about you? And you can't say Aurora. I just ate.

Ayden: Fine. My favorite thing is something that hasn't happened yet. A regular, normal, full length, uninterrupted by any morons, meaning you guys, demons, or near-death experiences…date with Aurora.

Matthias: I knew you were going to make me nauseous.

Ayden: Oh, shut up. Like you're favorite thing doesn't make everyone's skin crawl.

Blake: Yeah, dude. What is it? Figuring out how to get away with Aurora's murder?

Tristan: Building a death ray?

Logan: Stealing candy from babies?

Jayden: Deracinating appendages from papilionoidea?

The boys stare at Jayden

Ayden: I think he means pulling wings off of butterflies.

Jayden: That's what I said.

Blake: Sure dude.

Matthias: *rolls eyes* No, you nitwits. It's storytime with Selena and Bubbles.

Ayden: *sighs* Reading stories to an adorable five-year-old and her favorite stuffed platypus? I hate it when you show your softer side. Couldn't you just stick with the dark and brooding thing?

Logan: He always likes to make us look bad.

Matthias: Like that's hard.

Ayden: We can add it to his list of favorite things.

Matthias: Good idea. Natalie, thanks for putting up with us. It's been pleasure.

Blake: Can I stay for dinner? I want some of your awesome Irish cooking.

Logan: She already has four boys to deal with.

Blake: So what's six more?

Ayden: Including you? A big pain. Thanks Natalie, we're happy to visit anytime!

Blake: Can I at least get a hug?

Matthias: Get him out of here.

THE HEX BOYS

Host: Jenny

Today is a special day. It marks the return of the oh-so swoon-worthy Hex Boys to Supernatural Snark, and I couldn't be more excited to turn things over to them (well, really, they just sort of took over, but they're hot, so what's a girl to do but let them turn on all the charm and flirt?). I had the chance to ask the boys what one question they wish they'd be asked in an interview. A bit of chaos ensued. Enjoy!

Blake: There are so many questions you ladies could ask me but—

Logan: One question only, Blake.

Blake: That's good because there's only one thing I wish to be asked. I wish these gorgeous ladies would ask me out!

Ayden: *rolls eyes* Here we go.

Tristan: At least he's out of the way.

Blake: How about it Jenny? Let's ditch these fourth wheels and run off together. You're the answer to all my questions.

Jenny swoons

Matthias: *shoves Blake off Jenny* Nope, your turn is over. Jayden, you're up.

Tristan: What sciency mumbo-jumbo genius question do you want to answer?

Jayden: Actually, I would like to be asked questions of a romantic nature.

All Hex Boys: *Look stunned* What?!

Jayden: All the interviewers ask multiple questions of the rest of you regarding your romantic propensities, but for the rare times I'm interviewed, I'm scarcely given such queries. And never about my "dream girl."

Blake: Hate to break it to you, dude, but finding a chick that can keep up with you is going to be tough.

Jayden: She wouldn't have to be my exact intellectual equal. What I most value is acceptance of my "quirks," as you call them, a love of learning, and proficient social skills, which I lack. Once Ayden leaves, I would appreciate a companion who could continue my education on social conduct and help others connect with me.

Ayden: *looks anywhere but at his brother* You'd do just fine without me.

Jayden: The past has proven otherwise.

Blake: Remember that time Jayden was explaining to Aurora how many eggs she had in her flappy tubes.

Jayden: You mean her falo—

Logan: Don't correct him! Can we move on?

Ayden: Yeah, let's. I'm curious how many cars Logan's crashed.

Logan: With my skills, why would you think I'd crash any?

Ayden: That's not an answer.

Logan: It's all you're going to get. I wish I was asked where I'd like most to drive which would be the—

Blake: Isle of Man in Ireland.

Logan: Yes. They've got—

Jayden: No speed limits on rural roads.

Logan: And—

Ayden: A bunch of races every year.

Tristan: When you do talk, it's pretty much one of the only things you do talk about.

Logan: Well…it's cool.

Tristan: I'd like to be asked what we would cosplay together at—

Matthias: We are not dressing up in costumes with you.

Ayden: Seconded.

Blake: Wait, wait, could I be shirtless?

Logan: I'm out.

Tristan: Fine. I'd like to be asked what my dream girl and I would couples cosplay as.

Ayden: *coughs* Nerd! *cough, cough*

Tristan: *whacks Ayden* We'd do Spider Man/ Gwen Stacey or Dr. Who/Companion costumes that would look way better than anything you guys could pull off.

Blake: I already told you I'd pull off my shirt.

Ayden: I'd like to be asked where I'd take Aurora on our demon-death-injury free date.

Matthias: A prison cell is about the only place that could happen, mate. And you could leave her there locked up at the end.

Ayden: *punches Matthias's shoulder* Dinner and a movie has not worked out well. I was going to take her to Paris, but that's not a good idea anymore. She likes Italy, but that's a worse idea now. So I'd take her for dinner on our old sailboat out on the lake. Go to the remote side, water and forests for miles. Light some candles when it gets dark and the moon comes out—

Blake: Lame!

Matthias: *snorts*

Tristan: I think you've been watching too many chick-flicks with Blake.

Blake: I don't watch chick-flicks with Ayden!

Ayden: Yeah!

Blake: I watch them with Logan.

Logan: No! No we don't!

Jayden: I have often watched them with you and Blake.

Logan: I don't know what you're talking about. What's Matthias's question?

Matthias: Absolutely nothing. I don't want to be asked a bloody thing. *stands up* Thanks for having us. We'll be leaving now. *turns to leave*

Jayden: I would like him to be asked about the events surrounding when he gained his powers as a young boy.

Matthias: *freezes*

Ayden: Tread lightly, Jayden.

Jayden: Everyone wants an explanation of exactly what happened to his mother and—

lights go out

Jayden: Ow!

Ayden: Matthias, let him go!

Tristan: Ow, that's me!

Ayden: Sorry!

Blake: I've got Matthias!

Logan: You've got me.

Blake: Oh. Hey, is this shirt silk? Where can I get one?

Logan: You can get off of me.

Ayden: Does anyone have Matthias?

Jayden: I believe he vacated the premises.

AURORA

Host: Auggie

Please enjoy this tour featuring an AWESOME series and one of the most hilarious character interviews I've ever had the pleasure of participating in! One of the Hex Boys might have even brazenly flirted with me! ;) Check it out!

~Auggie

Auggie: So you're on the run from hell's minions and you've only got 15 minutes to stop and grab a bite to eat. What fast food joint are you going to swing by?

Aurora: In-N'-Out Burger. Fries, chocolate milkshake, and cheese burger with the works, because when running for my life, I burn enough calories to afford it. And all those carbs give me reason to live!

Auggie: A girl's always got to have ONE essential item with her at all times. What's yours?

Aurora: A back-up plan for when things go wrong. Because they always do.

Auggie: Everyone's going crazy to know more about the mysterious Hex Boys. Do you have a favorite? Anyone you're particularly drawn to?

Aurora: The Hex Boys are equal parts hot, hilarious, and hellacious fighters. They've had my back more than once, but a favorite? Blake put you up to that question, right? *glances around* I'm not stepping on that landmine. All of them are my favorite in different situations. Logan's patient and supportive when I suck at all this demon stuff. Tristan's worries a ton, but helps pull me back from extra stupid decisions. Jayden always tells the truth, I just need a dictionary to translate the genius's ridiculous vocabulary. Matthias is my favorite to mess because he's such a jerk and deserves it. And then there's Ayden…*sighs dreamily* He's hot literally and figuratively. So smooth, but can be awkward which is somehow adorably sweet. He's irritating when he's overprotective, but somehow sexy at the same time. He drives me crazy. In good ways. And bad. It's very confusing. And sexy. Did I mention that? And then there's Blake who even in the worst possible situations, makes us all smile. *looks over shoulder and raises voice* Which would make Blake my favorite!

Blake: *jumps out of hiding* I knew it!

Aurora: Oh my God. *gapes at Blake's barely there Spartan costume*

Ayden: *steps out not in costume* You idiot. She just said that to draw you out. Of course, I'm her favorite. Were you not listening? I'm sexy and adorable.

Blake: I heard irritating. Besides, she knew you were here too. She just said all that to save your delicate ergo.

Ayden: You mean ego. And it's not delicate.

Blake: It's sad that you're so illusional.

Ayden: Delusional!

Blake: *claps Ayden on the shoulder* Glad you can finally admit it, dude.

Ayden: *growls in frustration*

Aurora: *still gaping at Blake* What are you wearing?

Blake: *looks down at his broad chest and chisel abs before flexing incredible biceps* It's Halloween, babe. *taps silver helmet* Knight in shining armor.

Ayden: *pokes Blake's abs* But there's no armor.

Blake: *waves hand over self* Why would I want to cover this up?

Aurora: It's a Spartan cos— Nevermind. Why are you guys here?

Ayden: I just came to make sure he didn't bug you.

Aurora: *rolls eyes* Epic fail on that count. Steal my interview and I'm kicking you out.

Blake: I didn't plan on stealing your interview babe, just Auggie's heart.

Ayden: *gags*

Auggie: It's the end of the world and you can only listen to one more song. Which one is it?

Aurora: Staying Alive by the Bee Gees. It's old, like my parents who play it often and dance to it but that's another horror. I'd use it to get motivated because after all I've been through, I can figure out how to stop the end of the world.

Blake: She is good at getting out of impossible situations.

Ayden: After she gets herself, and us, in them.

Aurora: No one asked you. Moving on.

Auggie: How about giving us readers 3 important "never-forget" rules for living life on the run?

Aurora: Don't trust anyone.

Ayden and **Blake:** Hey!

Aurora: Unless it's a Hex Boy. Ditch anything electronic. It can be tracked.

Ayden: Yeah, that's how I tracked Blake here. Cell phone.

Blake: It's off.

Ayden: I'm that good.

Aurora: Tip three, always use cash. Tip four, change your appearance, tip five, avoid surveillance cameras—

Ayden: *eyeing Aurora with concern* Auggie only asked for three. Why do you know so much about this?

Aurora: Aunt M.

Ayden: *Shivers* Your crazy aunt is intense.

Blake: Do you still have her taser?

Aurora: If I did, I'd use it on you right about now.

Auggie: So we know that your life is constantly on the line. How do you relax on those really stressful days?

Ayden: Playing really bad croquet with her family.

Blake: And cooking with her mom. Or reading mythology books.

Ayden: Anything that doesn't involve leaving her house.

Aurora: I leave my house to do fun, relaxing things.

Ayden: Like what?

Aurora: Pssh, like... *scratches head* going to your house to...see if there are any new leads on the traitor trying to kill me. Okay, so maybe I need to do more fun stuff.

Auggie: Weapon of choice?

Aurora: My quick wit.

Ayden and Blake: No.

Aurora: Oh. *nods with confidence* Then my sharp detective skills.

Ayden: You're the worst detective ever! Remember when you thought we were trying to kill you?

Blake: Drug you?

Ayden: Sell you to human traffickers?

Aurora: *glares* Weapon of choice is anything sharp. Liking knives right about now.

Ayden*: *scoots back** See? Much scarier.

Blake: Babe does have killer knife throwing skills, but my skills with the ladies are much more interesting. I'm sure Auggie would love a demonstration.

Ayden: No, she would not.

Blake: But—

Aurora: Next question!

Auggie: Coffee or Tea?

Aurora: *smiles at Ayden* Coffee. Chocolate raspberry mocha.

Ayden: With cinnamon. Did you know it comes in sticks?

Blake: Dude, everyone knows that.

Auggie: Any advice for aspiring survivalists being chased by demon hell spawn?

Aurora: First, don't get chased by demon hell spawn. But if you're like me and that's impossible, you'd better hone your fighting skills, get in great shape so you can run to holy ground asap, and best of all, get a most awesome Hex Boy to help you out.

Blake: She means me.

Ayden: *Snorts* No way.

Blake: Enough with the jealousy. Let's face it. Besides running, I'm the only thing keeping babe alive.

Aurora: Hey, what about my own awesome powers? I'm dangerous.

Blake: Dangerously hot in those jeans!

Ayden: Give it up.

Blake: Never. But, you're right, as hostess with the mostest, Auggie deserves all my attention. *takes Auggie's hand* So lovely lady, how about you and I—

Aurora: Never meet again. Thanks so much for having us, Auggie. Ayden, little help?

Ayden: *dragging Blake out* Yeah, Auggie deserves much better than you.

Aurora: See? Best to have a Hex Boy around to help you out of disastrous situations. Especially when that disastrous situation is another Hex Boy. Blake being the worst.

Blake: *yells from outside* I heard that!

Aurora: But I just called you my number one. Number one worst, but still that makes you—

Blake: Your bestest worstest! Awesome! See little man? Told you I'm her favorite. Ow! Did Matthias not mention my safe word?

Aurora: Thanks for putting up with them, Auggie. Happy Halloween!

AURORA

Host: Danny

I have the most amazing post for you guys today!!! It's the funniest post and .. Hottest.. I'm having to share. So here is the thing. I absolutely LOVED Demons at Deadnight – the first book in this series. And … this might have included the fact that there are quite a few hot boys in the picture! The infamous Hex Boys!

You see, Aurora somehow ended up with these smoking hot boys to go and hunt demons!

So when thinking about Guest Posts for the tour, I asked the ladies about Tips from Aurora (the main character) about some tips to work with the Hex Boys!

And…well, let's say that the Boys wouldn't let Aurora alone on this one and completely took over, and…made me blush a few times too…

Aurora: Oh boy, tips on how to work with the Hex Boy's? I wish
I'd gotten the handbook. First thing you've got to understand

is that they have no concept of personal boundaries. In fact...lets give it five, four, three, two, and... *points at door*

Door opens

Logan: Hey, I respect personal boundaries. It's Blake that doesn't. Blake, come with me right now! Wait where is he?

Aurora: He's not here.

Logan: How did that happen? I was sure he was going to crash your interview.

Aurora: *Turns back to Danny* Tip two, know that the Hex Boys always travel in packs.

Danny: Oh I already heard all about this...

door opens again

Ayden: All right Blake, let's go. You've crashed enough interviews.

Logan: He's not here. Yet.

Ayden: How did we beat him?

Logan: *shrugs*

Ayden: *sits down beside Aurora* We'll wait and catch him when he shows up. Always nice to see you Danny. What's next, Aurora? Always stay close to the most smokin' hot Hex Boy?

Aurora: Are you ever going to let that go? *shakes head* Tip three, Matthias is a jerk and feel free to tell him so. Show weakness and he will own you.

Matthias: *walks in with whips coiled in each hand* Which means I've owned you forever. You show nothing but weakness.

Aurora: See? Jerk. Tell him often. On the upside, if you need a babysitter, he's your guy. My sister Selena adores him. But then again. She's five.

Matthias: Your whole family adores me.

Aurora: Only because they don't know you like I do.

Matthias: *rolls eyes* I wish you didn't know me at all. Where's Blake?

Ayden: Not here.

Logan: Yet.

Aurora: Tip five is to not let Ayden distract you with those dreamy eyes, sultry moves, and smokin' hot everything.

Ayden: *narrows eyes* Ok, what did you do?

Aurora: *Lowers voice* I'll tell you when Matthias isn't close enough to hear or yell at me. *turns to Danny* Oh, and if Ayden comes at you with handcuffs, run.

Ayden: That was one time and it was only to make sure you stayed put so you'd be safe.

Logan: But we ended up needing her help, which is what I told you guys.

Aurora: *smiles at Logan* Tip six, in tough situations, always ask Logan's opinion. He doesn't talk much, but his mind is like a steel trap always working out the best angles. *pats Logan's head* But don't flash to much skin or he'll faint. Tip seven, don't tell Blake a secret. Guy can't keep one. Tip eight, when Tristan panics, don't join in. It only makes things worse.

Tristan: *comes through door with Jayden* Just because I take the end of the world as we know it seriously, as you all should, doesn't mean I panic.

Matthias: Not helping your case there, mate.

Jayden: This is not an 'end of the world' situation. When Blake strove anew to deceive us into giving him Danny's abode, we concluded he planned to infringe upon your convocation so we came to repossess him.

Ayden: *smiles at everyone's confused looks* They came to get Blake.

Aurora: Tip nine, carry a thesaurus when you're with Jayden.

Ayden: I can translate him.

Aurora: But you're not always around.

Ayden: When are you alone with Jayden? Is he experimenting on you again?

Jayden: It was a single incident!

Aurora: Can I just point out to you geniuses that everyone but Blake is here.

Blake: *comes in through door* No, I'm here babe! Danny, you just keep getting more beautiful by the second.

Danny: *blushes furiously*

Aurora: *Snaps fingers and points at Danny* Tip ten, ignore Blake's flirting.

Blake: Impossible! Who would want to?

The Hex Boys all raise their hands

Blake: Always with the jealousy. Tsk tsk. Ignore them, Danny, and look what I got my gadget loving girl! *shows Danny small black metal disc in this hands* This is next, next generation chickadee. It's a Mandatum tracker! Keep it with you always.

Danny: *looks at the black metal disc quite confused*

Matthias: So you can follow her?!

Logan: *groans and drops face in hands* Oh, Blake.

Tristan: Don't take it, Danny!

Danny: *drops the weird metal box instantly*

Ayden: That's so creepy!

Aurora: Blake, we need to talk.

Jayden: Even I know that is wrong.

Blake: What? She can turn it on if she's ever in trouble and we can go save her.

Hex Boys and Aurora: Oh.

Blake: Jeez, you guys are such stalkers.

Matthias: You still can't leave Mandatum technology with her. *takes tracker from Blake* Sorry Danny, but it's for your protection.

Danny: Uhm.. I actually like to be safe. No?

Blake: But what if she gets into danger?

Danny: See?

Matthias: She won't. She's not stupid like Aurora.

Aurora: Smarter than you, Australia.

Matthias: Oh please.

Aurora: Escaped you. Twice. How's that bruise looking?

Matthias: That was luck and there's no bruise.

Aurora: Really? *stands up and reaches for Matthias* Let me check.

Matthias: No. *Dodges and backs out door.*

Aurora goes after him

Matthias: Ow! Ayden get your stupid nitwit off me!

Ayden: Like I can control her?

Aurora: Ow! Who hits a girl?

Matthias: You're not a girl.

Jayden: Not true. Her anatomical make-up consists of decidedly female components including a va—

Logan: No, no, no! *slaps hands over ears*

Jayden: *gives him a confused look* Including a variety of gender specific biological essentials which quantify her as muliebrous.

Aurora: *comes back in* Thank you. I think.

Ayden: I don't think it was much of a compliment.

Aurora: At least he called me a girl. So Danny, final tip for working with Hex Boys. Trust them. As annoying and nuts as they can be, if you're in a jam, especially the supernatural kind, there's nobody better at getting you out of it. Now, we'll get out of your hair. Thanks for having us!

Blake: See you guys later! *sits down and scoots closer to Danny*
So gorgeous, how about you and I—

Logan: Nope. *Grabs back of Blake's shirt and with Jayden's help
drags him out*

Tristan: Danny, sorry about…everything. We're usually much
better than this.

Jayden: No we're not.

Hex Boys: Shut up, Jayden!

Danny: *snickers* Thank you all so much for being here today!
Even though I only asked Aurora for some tips, I'm uhm..
grateful about all your insights too! and .. Blake, about
that…….

AYDEN

Host: Lori

Welcome to the final stop on the Divinicus Nex Chronicles Blog Tour! I'm super excited to have authors A & E Kirk and their larger than life characters taking over the blog today! Keep reading for an entertaining character interview!

Lori: Give us three interesting facts about you.

Ayden: I use my supernatural powers to hunt demons, I'm a great ballroom dancer, and in order to keep her safe, I'm hiding a certain redhead named Aurora from the secret society I work for. Which could get me killed, or at least branded as a traitor and...severely punished. But she's worth it.

Lori: Tell me about the place where you live.

Ayden: Gossamer Falls is a mountain town above Los Angeles. It got its name from the near constant fog and mist that covers the town. We've got a big lake, gorges, rivers, and amazing waterfalls.

Blake: With a secret cave behind one of the waterfalls that leads
    to—

Ayden: *jumps up and slaps hand over Blake's mouth* Something
    we don't talk about! What are you doing here?!

Blake: Seriously? Romancing the Dark Side? That has my name all
    over it. And Lori wants me all over her. Right, beautilicious
    babe?

Ayden: Don't encourage him.

Lori: Who is your best friend in the world and what is he/she like?

Blake: It's me.

Ayden: No.

Blake: That's fine because Lori's my best friend. Got to be friends
    before lovers, right?

Ayden: *cringes* I knew you were going to embarrass me. All the
    guys are my best friends. Except Blake right now. But my
    brother, Jayden, is my best, best friend.

Blake: Ouch. I speak for the other guys when I say that is deeply
    hurtful to hear. But I'll keep your secret if you disappear so
    Lori and I can get some time alone together.

Ayden: Between the two of us, it's not you she wants time alone
    with. *winks at Lori*

Blake: Are you flirting? You can't flirt! That's my intrusive
    territory.

Ayden: You mean exclusive.

Blake: That too.

Ayden: Although you are intrusive.

Blake: Told ya so.

Lori: What do you consider your special talent?

Ayden: Being smokin' hot.

Blake: This again? Are you ever going to let that go?

Ayden: Fine. Special talent? Understanding what Aurora's thinking even before she does.

Blake: Fair enough.

Ayden: And knowing that whatever she's planning is going to be a disaster.

Lori: Describe yourself to me in 140 characters or less.

Blake: I'll do it for him. Goofy, Dumbo—

Ayden: What are you talking about?

Blake: I'm describing you in fictional characters. Duh. Oh, Dopey, too. But I don't think I can come up with one hundred forty and yours are all lame anyway. Now for me, we can go with Superman, James Bond, Mr. Darcy—

Ayden: Not those kind of characters. Who's Dopey now*? *smiles at Lori* Let's go with: A demon's worst nightmare and a girl's hottest dream.

Blake: Gross! I'm gonna be sick. Next question already.

Lori: What's your biggest fear? You don't have to answer this one if you don't want to...

Ayden: Aurora or the guys dying in the midst of this chaos.

Blake: *gathers Ayden into hug* I'd be lost without you too, dude.

Ayden: *squirming* Get off! I never said that.

Lori: If you had a day to do anything you wanted, what would you do?

Blake: Spend every moment with you! Lori, please be mine!

Ayden: Blake, please get real. *shakes head* Anything? I'd go to Disneyland with family and friends. Even idiot Blake. Sounds lame but we never went because my parents were too scared that we'd attract demons and endanger people. Honestly, it wouldn't matter so much what I did, but that I could do it without looking over my shoulder or worrying about anticipating danger and demons around every corner. I guess I'd just love a day off demon duty.

Lori: What three things would you take to a Desert Island?

Blake: I just need a hot lady I adore, and Lori you're my number one choice!

Ayden: *snorts* For today. I'd be more inclined to take a working satellite phone, drinking water, and a knife.

Blake: Not Aurora? Babe's gonna totally be Team Blake after she hears that.

Ayden: Aurora's going to stay Team Ayden when she hears I wanted her safe at home instead of marooned on an island.

Lori: Quick, you get one wish…What did you just wish for? It's alright, you can tell me…

Blake: Lori to be my girlfriend. Did it work?! *moves toward Lori* Maybe it's like Aladdin's lamp and I need to rub—

Ayden: Hands off! *shoves Blake aside* I wish Aurora was safe from the society forever.

Matthias: *steps in with other Hex Boys* Really, mate? Because I'm thinking you wished for back-up.

Ayden: Second on my list. *sighs with relief* Thanks. He was getting out of hand.

Blake: Aw come on, guys! Let me have one gorgeous gal!

Logan: Not a chance.

Tristan: Yeah. We like Lori too much.

Lori: Anything else you feel like sharing?

Blake: My heart! My soul! My life! Lori, take me, I'm yours!

Ayden: Oh my God. *rolls eyes* Grab him.

Jayden: Yes, his prolix sycophancy prolific with plaudits seems to be straddling past cultural acceptance into the audacious. His behavior could besmirch our public esteem.

Matthias: *rubs his temples* Ayden, translation?

Ayden: Blake's acting like a lovesick idiot and could make us look bad.

Tristan: What else is new? We should go before it gets worse.

Lori: Thanks so much for taking some time to answer my questions today!

Ayden: *bows to Lori* Anytime. And it was my pleasure. Booklovers are among our favorite people. Logan?

Logan: Got him. *jumps on Blake's back and they disappear out the door in a mini tornado. The Hex Boys follow*

MATTHIAS P.O.V

Host: Paula

I am ecstatic to share a chapter with you from Demons At Deadnight! Now, the books are from Aurora's POV but this one is special because it's from *drum roll* MATTHIAS's POV. Ah, this guy is so cruel... I LOVE HIM! Let's see what the lovely authors got to say. Hello ladies!

Hello everyone! Thanks Paula for having us and giving us such a unique topic! For a short chapter from a Hex Boy's point of view, we thought we'd give Matthias a chance. We actually wrote this particular scene years ago when we thought about having sections of the book from the Hex Boy's point of view so it's a deleted scene from way, way back!

This scene is from Demons at Deadnight, before Aurora and the Hex Boys know or trust each other. Aurora gets ordered about by a demon threatening her family and must go off to meet him. What she doesn't know is that Matthias actually heard the demon and knows she's a dead damsel walking if she goes through with it.

****

"Aurora, wait," Matthias said forcing a genial tone into his voice. He'd show the guys he could be charming. "Where are you off to?"

Aurora faced him unable to completely squelch that deer-in-the-headlights look. "Left my homework at home. Funny, it being homework you'd think home would be where it's supposed to be but no, I need it at school, but you can't call it schoolwork because that's just stuff you do at school but it really is schoolwork that you do at home and then bring it back so you could call it school-home-school work but either way it's not here and I need to get it from home and get it to school so home is where I need to go now." She took a breath. "Bye."

Matthias shook off any attempts to make sense of her blabbering. "You should wait for your mum. Not go wandering off alone."

"That's sweet but I don't want to be late for school."

She backed another step and turned to leave. Toward her death. Matthias snatched her wrist and jerk her around. Be nice, he reminded himself, but didn't let go.

"I'm sure the teachers will let it slide." An oh-so-charismatic smile played on his lips. That seemed to terrify her further. She tried to wiggle free. His grip tightened. Why couldn't she make this easy? Did she want to get eaten alive? She really wasn't too bright.

Aurora chewed her lip so hard he expected blood. If she insisted on leaving he'd have to act as escort. Bloody hell.

She suddenly pressed herself onto his chest and sobbed pathetically. What the hell?

"This has just been so scary," she whimpered.

He still held one wrist but her other arm wrapped around him, pulling him tight and pressing their bodies close.

"This has been so scary!" she wailed. "And now," more sobbing, "and now," incoherent blubbering. She tightened her grip around him.

Matthias went rigid with shock, and released her wrist. "Uhhh."

"Now you're here and can help me, hold me!"

"What the—?" No, no, no. His arms reached out to his sides in a panic. The weeping girl clung to him. His mouth opened but no words surfaced. He pressed his lips together. One of his hands moved to pat her head but changed its mind and backed off.

As suddenly as she'd grabbed him, Aurora pushed off and sprinted down the street.

Matthias stared after her. He had to admit she was fast. She ducked around a corner and disappeared out of sight. His teeth ground hard enough to turn enamel to dust.

He'd been duped.

"Son of a—" His cell phone rang and he flipped it open with such force it almost snapped in half. "What?!"

"Jeez, what's wrong?" Ayden said.

"I had her but—"

Aurora's scream echoed and cut Matthias' answer short. He raced down the street and turned the corner. Empty.

He slammed a palm into a building and shouted into the phone, "She's gone!"

"Aurora?"

"Yeah. I had her and now she's gone."

"She got away from you?" Ayden said.

A grizzly would have cowered at the growl that crawled out of Matthias's throat.

Ayden chuckled. "Oh, I can't wait to hear this."

***

There you go! Now you know why he was being weirdly nice to her. Maybe Aurora wouldn't have been so creeped out if she knew! Although, it is Matthias. Him being nice, always creeps her out.

Thanks for having us!

AURORA'S PROFILE

Host: Alicia

NAME: Aurora Lahey
AGE: 17
HAIR: Red
EYES: Blue
HEIGHT: Tall, leggy

SUPERNATURAL ABILITIES:

~ Psychic visions that give her the ability to track demon locations. She considers it the crappiest superpower on the planet.

SKILLS:

~ Running, hiding, quick wit, snarky humor, knife throwing.

LIKES:

~ Her family, ice cream, chocolaty anything, running for exercise, The Discovery Channel, mythology, Van Helsing (her cat), Hex Boys (minus Matthias)

HATES:

~ Celery, Waiting World, demons, her brothers and sisters stealing her chocolate, running for her life, Matthias Payne, insane asylums, trusting strangers, dogs.

BACKGROUND:

Aurora was born and raised in Gossamer Falls by Gemma and Clyde Lahey. She has a very close family with two younger sisters and two younger brothers. At the age of eight, her parents moved the family to the Los Angeles area after Clyde Lahey received a prominent surgeon position.

Not long after, Aurora began seeing monsters, visions of demons lurking around the corner. Aurora told her parents about the creatures only once and upon realizing they could not see the monsters, never mentioned them again. Gemma and Clyde chalked up Aurora's fear to her active imagination of the boogie man. Aurora learned all she could about the monsters she saw and put those diligent studying skills toward being a good student. Even founding and chairing a club in high school.

In her junior year of high school, while touring a college during a school field trip, Aurora was attacked and nearly murdered. Left for dead, she would have died had a stray cat not sat beside her and created enough noise to draw the attention of local residents. Aurora adopted the cat and called him Van Helsing. Her parents moved the family back to Gossamer Falls seeking a safer town to raise their children.

The night before Aurora's first day at Gossamer Falls a demon deviates from the norm of ignoring Aurora and instead tried to kill her. To complicate matters further, she's slammed with an unpleasant first interaction with the Hex Boys, six hot hunks with dark pasts and dangerous futures. Further contact with them only gets her lies, thievery, home-invasions, a headache whenever Matthias Payne shows up, and a flustered blush in Ayden Ishida's presence.

Now she juggles danger, demons, growing desires and supernatural skills while trying to keep her grades up and evade those who want to kill or kidnap her.

Piece of cake, right? She really only has one daily goal.

Survival.

AYDEN & TRISTAN P.O.V

From us via the February 2015 Hexy Knight Newsletter

As a Valentine's Day gift to you, here are two scenes from the very beginning of Demons at Deadnight which are from Ayden's and Tristan's point of view. The first occurs while Aurora is first being chased home by the flying demon. The second scene happens a short time later, after Aurora has her first encounter with the two boys then Luna has called Aurora in to dinner, leaving Tristan and Ayden alone in the front yard. Hope you enjoy!

SCENE 1

Ayden had decided to walk the quiet streets rather than drive to Tristan's house to give himself time to come up with some answers but that wasn't going well. It still didn't make sense.

Demons escaped from hell but they never came here. Not willingly anyway. Hanging around in this town put their life in danger. Not life since a demon was technically already dead. But if you go to all the trouble to mutilate, torture and eat your way out of hell, make it through a portal and onto earth, it only made sense that you would get as far away as possible from the hunters waiting to send you back.

So why did the demon come here at all? And why did it continue to linger? What did it want? He didn't have answers. None of them did. The situation was troublesome.

Maybe Tristan had put some pieces together. He pulled out his phone, but an inhuman screech blasting through the dwindling sunlight stopped him mid-dial. The sound caught him off guard, and his body's visceral reaction was instantaneous, a fact that he promptly cursed. He took a deep breath and searched his surroundings, glad to find no one in the streets or peering out a window who could have witnessed his lack of control.

His relief quickly shifted to irritation when he looked at the phone in his hand, now nothing but a glob of melted metal trying to ooze through his fingers.

"Oh, great. Not again." He closed his hand to consolidate the goo and chucked it over his shoulder, already running by the time it landed with a wet splat on the sidewalk, molding itself into the cracks of the concrete as it cooled.

SCENE 2

After they watched Aurora disappear into the house, Tristan started a few sentences that began with things like, "What the...?" "How did she...?" and "Why didn't it...?" but each time his voice trailed off into uncertainty. Then he said, "What was with all the flirting?"

Ayden snorted. "I wasn't flirting."

"Sure you weren't, Captain Underwear." Tristan jutted out his hips suggestively and deepened his voice to an over-the-top, mocking version of sexy. "As for boxers or briefs, I'd be happy to show you, Aurora, new girl in town I'm trying to impress with how hot I am."

"I think she already noticed."

"What's that supposed to mean?"

Dark eyes narrowed, Ayden stared where he's last seen the redhead. "Does she seem familiar to you?"

"Familiar? We just met her." Tristan folded his arms. "Okay, what's going on with you?"

Leather creaked as Ayden rolled a shrug. "Not sure yet, but you'd better call Matthias. Tell him we've got a problem."

Tristan ran both palms across his temples and laced his fingers behind his head. "He is not going to be happy."

"He's never happy. Deal with it."

"You call him then." When Ayden didn't respond, Tristan looked his friend up and down. "Where's your phone?"

A pause. "Don't ask."

Tristan's arms slapped against his sides. "Again?"

"Just make the call."

MATTHIAS P.O.V

DROP DEAD DEMONS SCENE

Matthias didn't anticipate the library being so crowded. The high ceilings seemed to amplify the hushed conversation of students. Which intensified once he walked in. One cold look from the Australian, and his peers quickly averted their eyes, but he knew it wouldn't stop them from eavesdropping.

Luna stopped shelving books to wave from across the space. He flicked a hand in her direction. Her little "rep change" had drawn far too much attention as of late.

From the cell phone he held to his ear, someone laughed and said, "Selena broke someone's nose?!"

"Yes," Matthias snapped, then realized he spoke too loudly. He ducked his head down and moved quickly for the back of the library.

No one was ever in Gossamer Falls' local history section. It was dark, windowless. The seclusion should have made it attractive to the students, but there was an unsettling air that permeated the space and had them avoiding it for years.

"Why are you not more excited about this? Oh, are you still in the office?" his caller said.

"No." Matthias slipped into the secluded room and shut the door. "I just left the principal's office."

"So you're not in trouble. Then why are you upset? Is Selena hurt?"

He took a deep breath and lowered his voice. "She's fine, but—"

"Then your training with her paid off."

Matthias paced off his pent up energy. "Yes, the training worked, but now it's a big spectacle and..."

"I wouldn't worry about it. No one's going to blame you. In fact, you helped save the day."

"I don't know," he grumbled.

"I do."

"But—"

"No buts," the caller said firmly. "Some little boy trying to kiss her is just guy hormones. You've heard about those, right?"

"Uh-huh," Matthias rolled his eyes.

"This wasn't your fault. You're more of a hero than you think. Or want anyone else to think. But Selena's on to you, and no doubt feeling all kinds of proud of herself. Most important, she's safe."

"Right." Safety was the goal.

Plus Selena had defended *herself*, which was a vitally important ability when she had a sister who had demons trying to kill her every five minutes. Aurora, the walking disaster area, who sucked everyone close to her into the danger zone. It was just a matter of time before someone got seriously hurt.

"This was normal kid stuff," said the caller.

Sure, it wasn't demon related *this time*, but what about the next time, or the one after—

"Hey." The caller cut into his thoughts. "It isn't the same as your sister. You should be happy. Take Selena home yourself. It'll make you feel better."

Matthias relaxed his shoulders. Actually, he already did feel better. "You're right. Thanks."

"You're welcome." Then the caller chuckled. "The only thing you have to worry about is Blake being jealous that you honed in on his territory and saved the damsel."

Matthias suddenly noticed the muted squeak of sliding skin, purposefully shallow breaths, and a wriggling shadow on his back.

He grabbed a book off a shelf and whirled around, flinging the thick hardcover at the lurker. His aim was spot on, shooting directly at the spy's forehead.

But she had anticipated the attack and dropped to the ground. Pain scrunched Aurora's face as she landed on her butt.

"Bloody hell!" Matthias jumped back. How had he not noticed her? Guess that training was paying off. Her drop hadn't been graceful, not that she ever was, but she'd managed to dodge the blow. "Are you following me?"

"Of course not." Aurora rubbed her behind and pushed to her feet. "Be quiet or Caviezel will have us both in detention."

Matthias glanced over his shoulder. Mrs. Caviezel didn't take kindly to cell phones in *her* library. He didn't need Aurora seeing it either. He ducked the phone behind his back.

He saw her notice so decided to attack in order to deflect her attention. "Then what are you doing here?"

Her eyes widened slightly in panic. She said quickly, "Nothing. What are *you* doing here?"

"Nothing." Behind his back, Matthias's hand tightened around the phone.

Aurora studied him. He could see her scrambling.

"Who's on the phone?" she asked.

Crap. Now he was scrambling. "My...uh...dad." He brought the phone around and spoke into it. "I'll have to call you back...*Dad*."

"What?" his caller snorted. "Is this one of your jokes?"

Matthias scowled at the nitwit across the room. "No, I'm with Aurora."

"Ohhh," the voice said knowingly. "You're *with* Aurora. I see."

"What?"

"I thought there was a spark between you two."

"I'm not *with* Aurora."

"Don't fight it. Hate and love are really just two sides of the same coin. It was just a matter of time before you flipped that shiny new penny."

"Don't be—"

"Have your fun lover boy."

Aurora said, "Is that a new phone?"

"No!" Matthias snapped. "Same phone. The only one I have. Why would I have a second phone?"

The caller purred in his ear, "Because you're up to something very naughty."

What a bloody nightmare. Matthias clenched his jaw and lifted the phone away from his ear.

Aurora cocked her head. "I happened to get a good look at your phone when you were out cold last night and that's not it."

Well, wasn't she Miss Observant. And he didn't need reminding about last night when she'd actually gotten the drop of him. So humiliating.

"You're wrong. Moron," he said. "It's the only phone I have."

A phone rang. Matthias's *other* phone, his regular phone, in his jacket pocket. Maybe Aurora didn't notice.

Aurora smirked.

Of course she noticed.

He closed his eyes and sighed, chin dropping to his chest. This was not his day. Aurora would never let this go. She'd nag him with a constant barrage of questions about the "mysterious" phone until she got to the bottom of it. And what if she told everyone else? He had to figure out how to fix this. She could *not* have leverage on him.

Matthias spoke into the first phone, "Gotta go."

"Enjoy your date!"

He strangled back a growl and shoved the phone in his pocket before taking the other one out. "What!"

"Aurora never showed up for class." It was Ayden, frantic and out of breath. "I still can't find her. The other guys don't know where she is. I thought she ran again, but her backpack is in her locker. Rose must have gotten past our security. I'm such an idiot! I wasted almost an hour searching for her here, but that freaking psycho probably has her out of town by now and—"

"Wait, Ayden," Matthias smiled. Oh, how the tables had turned. This was going to be good. "What was that about Aurora? She *ditched* you, and you don't know where she is? That's interesting because I think I might be able to help you out with that."

Aurora's face fell, skin paling.

"*Ditched* me?" Ayden said, confused. "Who said she ditched me?"

Aurora waved her hands and shook her head whispering, "I'm not here!"

Matthias pressed the phone to his chest and whispered, "And I don't have another phone, right?"

"Fine," she scowled. "No second phone."

Heh, heh, heh. Maybe it was his day. Matthias put the phone to his ear.

Ayden was ranting, "—not the time for one of your 'I told you she's a bloody idiot' moments."

"Yeah, I found her," Matthias said.

Aurora's jaw dropped, and she stomped her foot. "Really?"

He rolled his eyes, stifling a smile. This was too much fun. "She's in the library."

"Be right there," Ayden said with quiet fury. "I'll deal with her when I take her to P.E."

Aurora looked like she was about to explode.

Matthias struggled to keep from laughing. He hated for it to end, but... "She didn't ditch you. Luna needed her help. Everything's fine. Go to class. I'll make sure she gets to P.E."

"But—"

Matthias hung up on him and studied Aurora. "Do I need to know what you're doing here?"

"No," Aurora said too quickly, her voice squeaking with anxiety. She brushed past him. "But you might want to check out a certain alcove on the second floor. I think something of Flint's still lives."

"Great," he groaned. And we were back to her being a pain. "What did you do now?"

"It wasn't me."

"It never is." He followed her out of the library thinking, *Except when it* always *is.*

As they headed down the hall, Aurora shot him an irritated squint over her shoulder. "I can get there myself."

Of course she *could*, but he knew she didn't plan to. Matthias flicked a dismissive "keep going" gesture.

Bollocks. He'd have to go back and check out the library to try to determine what she was up to. For the last few weeks he and the Hex Boys couldn't have gotten her out of their hair if they'd tried, and the truth was, she'd been doing pretty well being honest lately so...

Rose must have spooked her this morning. Have something on her. But what? Had they met before? Did she have more supernatural encounters than she let on?

She was still so skittish. And talk about the frigging walls she'd built to protect herself. Almost as sturdy as the mighty fortress he'd constructed around himself.

Crap.

He hated it when something she did made him "introspective." Hell, he hated the word "introspective" because it just brought up a whole bunch of useless feelings and memories that were best buried. It never helped.

She was *such* a pain.

He wished she'd just go away. Didn't he have enough on his plate? But like it or not, he'd protect her. Just like he protected the rest of the guys. And he'd protect them *from* her if need be, but first he had to figure out just what she was up to. He was a professional. He'd investigate.

Ugh. Like he had time for this. Why couldn't she just be honest?

Aurora flung her hair over her shoulder and smiled at him.

Creepy.

"Just can't get enough of me, huh?" she said. "First the kidnapping then following me to the library and now the gym."

"I didn't...do any of that." There was no way she believed this fantasy.

"Jeez, Matthias. I get it. You adore me."

Matthias snorted. "You are a certifiable loon." And trying to tick him off.

It was working.

"But you keep following me which just proves how deeply you've fallen for—"

The lights went out. The walls and floors shuddered and groaned, like the entire building was some stone giant waking from a deep slumber.

Matthias blinked twice before his powers adjusted and he could see clearly in the black. People screamed and raced around in the total darkness of the windowless hallway. A guy barreled their direction, arms striking out wildly for something solid to hang onto.

Matthias grabbed Aurora tight against him and shoved forward into the wall. The kid stumbled past them, but not before landing a fist on Matthias's back. Ow.

"Get off!" Aurora punched at Matthias's chest.

Ow! Well, Blake's weight training with her had been effective—her fist clipped his jaw. Ow!—and the boxing lessons too. What was she thinking?! Now she was trying to get away from him? Not happening.

He squeezed Aurora tight to squelch her struggles. "Shut it! Stay still!

She did. The school rocked again. There was no place to hide from the fear ridden hoard. Several students fell. The ones that didn't ran blindly in the direction they hoped to find doors. A few panicked kids came staggering their way, arms out and waving like a bunch of zombies as they stomped on fallen students.

Matthias grabbed the wrist of the closest idiot and shoved him hard, adding a kick to the chest to send him flying into the rest of the herd. They dropped like pins in a bowling alley. Strewn on the floor, they couldn't stampede over anyone else.

Aurora squirmed. "Did you do this?"

"No." His head swiveled as he searched for more stampeding morons. Aurora kept squirming against him. Really? Did she have to make everything harder? "I said *stay still.* "

"Then quit moving your head. Your hair is tickling my nose. It's getting really long."

He cringed. Was he really *that* close to her? "Well sor-*ry,* but I'm scanning for threats trying to save your worthless hide."

"If it's so worthless why are you trying to save it?"

Damn good question. "Because I'm an idiot."

"Finally, we agree."

He gritted his teeth. He really had a mind to walk away.

Someone bumped into his back. A quick kick knocked the culprit down. Just a student. As more of them struggled to their feet, Matthias contemplated using his whips to tether everyone down.

Aurora sniffed. "Are you wearing cologne?"

Really? Building possibly collapsing, teenagers stomping each other to death, and his cologne was what caught her attention? He would never understand what went on in that warped head of hers. But at least she had good taste in something. It was his favorite, because—Oh for the love of… She was so distracting.

He needed to focus. "Shut—"

The school stilled. Lights came on. Matthias blinked rapidly to adjust. The crazed crowd froze, looked around with anticipation, then as the lights stayed on, they relaxed. Someone starting hooting, others clapped.

What a bunch of brainless gnats. Just because things were fine now didn't mean they should celebrate and let their guard down. To Aurora's credit, she hadn't moved or slipped into the cheering spirit, but that was probably only because of her recent training.

Some Amazon girl backhanded Matthias's shoulder. "Jeez, you two. Get a room."

He frowned, looked at Aurora, and realized he was nose-to-nose with her. Bugger all. Did someone think they were together? As in…making out? Could this day get any worse? The only good news was that Aurora's face was a mask of revulsion that mirrored his own. Swallowing hard, he shoved away and scanned the hall.

"What was that?" Aurora asked.

"Don't know, but I don't like it. I'll get Blake or Jayden and check it out." He'd had enough of her and this entire day. And it wasn't even lunch. He grabbed her bicep, which had some impressive muscle tone—not that he'd tell her—and pushed her down the hall. "Right after I drop you off."

It was Logan's turn to babysit her.

They didn't get far before Aurora said, "Why don't you go take care of it now? Could be serious. I can get myself to P.E."

Matthias narrowed his eyes. All that and she still wanted to get back to sneaking off on her own? Must be important. What was her connection with Rose?

"Just keep moving." He dug his fingers into her back and shoved her forward.

"Ow!" Aurora grabbed her calf, hopped a few steps to the side and leaned on the wall. "Shoot. Must have pulled something when I fell in the library."

Oh, please. Matthias rolled his eyes. Not that she noticed. She was very focused on rubbing her leg.

"But, hey," she said, "don't let me slow you down. Get the guys and take care of things. I'll, uh, rest a minute then get to the gym. Unless," Aurora reached out and grasped his wrist looking all kinds of pathetic, "you want to carry me the rest of the way?"

Wow. She was really trying to work this. He looked at the hand on his arm, then back at her. She thought she was so clever. He clenched his jaw to help keep a straight face.

"I don't think so." He shook her off. "You can manage."

"Yeah, sure. You go...save stuff."

Oh, man, she was something else. He almost laughed, so he turned quickly and walked away. Now he could at least smile. Did she really think he'd fall for same lame trick twice? It worked out horribly for her with that flying demon, but this time he didn't care if she ran off and got herself killed.

He really didn't.

He stopped.

No. Just keep walking. Let her fend for herself. He didn't care.

He sighed. But the other Hex Boys would, and then they'd try to save her, put themselves in danger, and disaster would ensue. He could almost feel the steam coming out of his ears.

He turned around. Aurora was grinning all stupid and triumphant. That needed to stop. He scooped her up, a surprised grunt escaping her lips.

Matthias smirked. "Not this time."

She glowered. "Think you're so smart."

Yeah, I do, and I'm definitely..."Smarter than you." He headed down the hallway.

She wiggled and twisted. "Let me down."

He tightened his hold. "Oh, no. You wanted to play this game. Let's play." And let's play *big*. He picked up his pace and pushed through the crowd booming his voice loud so it bounced off the walls and caught everyone's attention. "Excuse me! Watch out! Coming through."

"I hate you," she muttered under her breath.

Matthias grinned with genuine pleasure. The locker room was in sight, and he'd ruined her day. A win-win.

"I said I'd get you to P.E. and now," he shouldered open the door to the girls' locker room, swung her back for power then threw her in, "you're at P.E. Whatever you do from here, don't make it my problem."

Aurora thudded on her butt. Again. That had to hurt. He smiled broader then turned on his heel as the girls' locker room door shut and pulled out his cell phone.

Something thumped against the door. He paused.

From inside the locker room, he heard Aurora say, "Jerk."

"He is so cool," some girl said.

Matthias chuckled. That had to irritate Aurora. He shook out his arms – the dimwit was heavier than she looked – and dialed his phone.

Logan answered on the first ring. "It wasn't Blake."

"What?" Matthias said.

"The school shaking? The blackout?"

He sighed and climbed a flight of stairs. "That's not what I'm calling about. Our village idiot is up to something."

"I don't think so," Logan said. "I usually know when Blake is—"

"Not him. *Aurora.*"

"Oh. I know. Already on it."

Matthias paused. "Well…good. Stay on her. Keep me updated and— Why didn't you tell me she was up to something?"

"Uh, because…"

The call disconnected.

Matthias growled and sent a quick text before ascending onto the third floor, and hurried down in the empty halls. He wasn't sure what was going on, but he was sure Aurora was responsible. Somehow. It probably started with the alcove where she thought "something of Flint's still lives." Leave it to her to activate a psychopath's dormant-until-now lethal technology.

She'd said alcove, but that could be a broom closet for all he knew, so when he reached the floor he started checking every door.

First one was locked. That wasn't a problem. A quick check to ensure the hall was empty, then he focused his energy down on the darkness of his own shadow. It warped and stretched beneath the door then rode up the inside until it found the handle. Matthias twisted his own hand. The shadow inside mimicked the movement and the door opened.

He nudged the door wider with his boot. Janitor supplies. He used his shadow to unlock the doors as he moved down the hall. The next door opened to dusty boxes. The next had paper supplies. The one after that had broken chairs. The door after that—

Didn't open. Which he realized too late as he walked headlong into it. An irritated noise rumbled up his throat as he rubbed his forehead. On the other side of the door, he worked his shadow again and twisted the handle. It didn't budge.

This had to be it.

He stepped back and kicked at the door. "Stupid Aurora and her stupid—Agh!"

The door swung open before Matthias's foot made contact. His arms pin-wheeled to no avail. He tumbled through the entry and crashed onto the floor.

"What the bloody hell?!"

"Sorry dude!" Blake rushed into the doorway. A flick of the big guy's wrist kept the door from banging into him. "Opened it for you. Thought I was helping."

Matthias scowled as Blake grasped the Aussie's hand and hauled him up.

"Is that what you texted me for?" Blake said. "A little breaking and entering? Because I didn't rock the school. I mean, obviously, I *rock* this school. But I didn't—"

"Shut it!" Matthias held up a hand for quiet as he scanned the dark alcove. "Do you sense anything in here that doesn't belong?"

Blake squinted his eyes and surveyed the area. After a moment he said, "You?"

Matthias gritted his teeth and sighed. Today, his patience was being sorely tested.

"So, hey, dude, why aren't we in class? Not that I mind. Although, I did snag a spot next to some pretty fine ladies. Or should I say, *they* snagged a spot next to *me*. I'm like honey to flies. Really pretty flies. More like honey to butterflies."

Matthias ignored him to tap on the walls, run fingers over the grooves in between stone. It all seemed normal. Nothing "alive." Daft as Blake was, he wouldn't be so cavalier if he sensed something serious. Aurora was probably overreacting, jumping to conclusions. How many times had that happened? Too many. But apparently he was the only one who noticed.

"What?!" Blake said.

He turned to find Blake on his cell phone, all good humor wiped from his friend's face. Matthias felt an icy dread. It took a lot to get rid of Blake's smile.

His own phone buzzed in his pocket. A brief check filled him with renewed tension. It was a notification from the portal's security system.

Blake finished his call, eyes wide, body on hyper-alert. "Logan and Aurora got kidnapped through a secret door by robots!"

"*Wh-what?!*" Matthias sputtered.

"That's what Ayden said!" Blake took off down the hall.

Matthias stepped into the hall and called out, "Ayden said *'robots'*?"

"We gotta save them!" Blake turned to skip sideways down the hall, waving frantically for Matthias to follow. "Come on!"

"You go." Matthias held up his cell phone. "The portal is about to open."

"No it's not." Blake skidded to a stop and checked his cell. "I'd have gotten a— crap."

"Get Jayden." Matthias backed away. "Then you two help Ayden."

Blake shifted uncomfortably then reversed and followed Matthias. "I'll go with you."

"No, I can handle the portal by myself."

"But what if something big and bad comes through the portal? What if it's more robots? What if you get sucked in? We never go alone. It's the rule. It's *your* rule."

Yes, he knew it was his rule, but sometimes rules needed to be broken because…"Logan and Aurora are more important. Go."

Blake grinned. "Did you just say Logan *and Aurora?*"

Ah, man. Blake had better not repeat that. Matthias rolled his eyes and sprinted away. "Go! That's an order!"

***

As the last door to the portal swished open, steam swallowed Matthias whole. He slid to a stop on the damp earth as the doors swished close behind him. The mist was so thick he could barely see across the cavernous space. The pool near the center boiled and bubbled steam like a vat of toxic waste. Matthias coughed on the wet, hot air and waved off the mist.

What was with this heat? It was like a sauna. The pool was usually placid, other than the liquid dripping onto the surface from the stalactites above. It'd never acted like a Jacuzzi before.

The security system hadn't reported an official opening yet, but…

His gaze swept the space carefully looking for any demons or monstrous shadows lurking where they shouldn't be. Times like these it would be handy to be the Divinicus Nex. No wondering if demons waited in the dark. You'd just know.

Ca-chunk, ca-chunk.

Matthias jumped as a metal net started to drop from the ceiling to cage in the portal. Good. All was working as it should. The net, invented by Flint, automatically lowered when there was an imminent threat of the portal opening and a demon coming through. So that event could happen any second.

Adrenaline *th-thumped* through his body, sending him into high alert, fingers trembling.

He stripped off his jacket and flung it to the ground, wiping sweat off his brow. He wasn't scared, but seeing the things that come out of Hell was always unsettling. He had to be ready for anything.

He flicked a long black shadow from one hand. He expected the usual routine.

The portal would stretch like a hand trying to push out of a balloon before a demon popped through into our world with a wet *clap!* With the creature trapped behind the metal net, Matthias would use his shadows to disintegrate the hellion, then he'd stroll back to school to fix whatever chaos Aurora had wrought.

He waited for the portal to swirl, which would start its transformation into something much more pliable than rock. It usually didn't take long to—

With a booming *crash!* the portal shattered as if made of glass. Matthias ducked and covered his hands over his ears as a huge monstrosity burst through the solid stone. The ground shook, water sloshed in violent waves over the sides of the pool.

The massive beast spun a graceful arc through the air and headed directly into Flint's net. Matthias let out a breath of relief and readied his whip, waiting for the net to catch it. But with a shriek of tearing metal, the cage ripped away like it was tissue paper. The demon exploded through.

Matthias froze, stunned. "No bloody wa—hungh!"

One of the metal strips bent back and slammed Matthias in the gut. At the impact, he flew back and rolled out on the dirt. The whole cavern quaked when the beast's front feet landed. Mist blasted away from the body in curling torrents.

Matthias winced and clutched his stomach as he sat up. His hand came away wet with blood, revealing a ragged tear in his shirt and several cuts across his torso. They were shallow, but it stung. Especially with the humid heat causing so much sweat. He glowered at the demon. Its long body slithered out of the gaping hole in the net. Big as a bus, multiple sets of glowing yellow eyes, long fangs, bones falling off its striped fur.

And worst of all, it was free.

It roared. A shrill howling noise that rattled the stalactites so hard, several broke off and torpedoed into the pool with loud, wet *plops.*

Still down, Matthias slammed his palms onto the stone floor. The demon's shadow lurched off the ground on either side and wrapped over its long body. A pull of Matthias's arms tightened the shadows and flattened the demon to the ground as it screeched in protest, the many rows of spindly legs scrambling.

Matthias gritted his teeth and readied for another pull, one that would slice all the shadows through the demon leaving it diced and disappearing into a black mist back to Hell.

The demon bellowed again and with a great heave, shoved itself up. The shadows ripped off and recoiled back to lifeless gloom.

Matthias' jaw dropped. That had never happened before.

The *one time* he went to the portal by himself and some crazed, caterpillar thing with exceptional powers comes through? Aurora's fault. Had to be.

The demon sniffed the air, noticed the bones which had dropped from its fur, and promptly inhaled them in one gulp. It sniffed again, saw Matthias, and careened directly at him. Matthias clambered to his feet. The ground trembled worse with every step as the demon gained speed. The bloody fangs were as long as his forearm.

Spittle sprayed from the demon's mouth. The stench made him gag. Matthias flung an arm in the air. Shadows dropped from above and knifed down in front of him acting like a shield.

Whap!

The demon's tongue slapped against the shadow shield, saliva drooling down. But through the loosely woven shadows, drool sprayed in wet globs that spattered Matthias's shirt.

"Ugh!" He turned away from the slime and the stench.

The demon sniffed the shield. Matthias opened his hands. From the shadow lines that created the shield, spikes lanced out and stabbed the creature's nose. It jerked back with an eardrum shattering squeal.

Matthias yelled, "Try that again you crazy bugger!"

The beast wheeled away, scampering for the other end of the cave.

"Coward," he snorted.

He threw his arms forward and his shadow speared ahead, ever thinning until it was two thick ropes. The shades lassoed over and over around the demon's head, and as Matthias yanked, the demon jerked off its feet with a surprised grunt.

Matthias smiled, then fisted his hands around the ropes for a final decapitating wrench. "Oh no you don't! I'm—"

The demon offered a short growl before tossing its head. Still holding the ropes, Matthias was flung into the air. He twisted, saw the ground coming, and tucked his head, landing on his shoulder. He rolled out of it and up into a deep side lunge.

"Ow! Bollocks!" Matthias snarled. "Now you asked for it!"

His movements caused the steam to swirl and billow, obscuring his vision, but he quickly spotted the rows of yellow eyes directly in front of him. Getting closer.

A clawed antenna knifed through the mist. Matthias leapt into several back-handsprings, moving out of harm's way until...

His body jerked. He heard a rip. Pain lanced his shoulder, and in the last back-handspring his arm gave out. He thudded hard on the dirt, clutching his shoulder. The blood was scarce, the cut superficial. But it stung. Just like his stomach. He hoped the saliva didn't have some poison seeping into his bloodstream. Well, if that was the case, before he dropped dead, he'd better drop this ugly bugger.

He pushed up to his knees, shadows collecting in his hands like dozens of writhing serpents. "You bloody son of a— Ugh!"

The demon's long, pointy nose caught under Matthias's stomach and flung him several feet. He shook his head to clear it, but in his blurry view, the world still trembled. He sat up, ready to defend himself again, but the demon was running away, head down, charging at one of the walls.

The demon rammed headlong into the stone. The ferocious impact shuddered the ground. Dust clouded. Pieces of rock flung through the air and pinged harmlessly off Matthias. The demon staggered back and shook its head. Then it took a deep, rumbling breath and charged the wall again.

Matthias stared. "What the hell?" It was trying to get out. That thing would ravage the town!

He flung a fast arm. A shadow shot out and slung a noose around three rows of legs. When Matthias wrenched his arm back, the noose pulled tight, The demon shrieked and fell, chin cratering the dirt, but then it twisted in a frantic fit and swung its head, chomping on the shade holding its legs, and the shadow rope disintegrated.

Matthias started to stand, but was knocked back down as the demon headbutted the wall again. Cracks spidered out from the impact. Chunks of rock fell away and left a deep concaved depression in the stone.

The demon charged once again, and finally, with a mighty, earth quaking *crack* the wall shattered, and the demon stumbled through. Metal shrieked and *clanged.*

Matthias grunted to his feet and ran. That *thing* was not getting away and doing a Godzilla number on Gossamer Falls.

"Logan, shoot!" Aurora screamed.

"What the—" Matthias muttered in shock then stumbled as panic skipped his heart.

Through the hole, he saw Logan facing down the demon. His face and clothes were filthy, his white hair matted with dirt and streaked with blood, but the smallest of the Hex Boys stood his ground and shot a slew of arrows. A true David and Goliath moment.

Because Logan never missed, all the arrows were direct hits, but they all glided harmlessly off of the demon.

Crap. This thing was practically indestructible. *Of course* it was going after Aurora. And it was going to kill both her *and* Logan in the process.

Matthias sprinted faster, because freaking Logan would not move! Instead of running, Logan stood and readied more arrows. He didn't know what he was up against.

"No!" Matthias shouted in a harsh, guttural command, then opened his arms wide, and with arms locked straight, brought his palms together.

As the *clap* resonated, every dark crevice of the cavern surged together and rocketed up and over his body. The wave of endless black twined over and over until four thick ropes whipped out around the demon. A shadow jumped from the ground to lasso Matthias's waist and tether him into the solid rock.

The demon jerked to an abrupt halt as the shadows pulled taut, cinching a hot pain around Matthias's gut and arms. He grunted, but shoved the hurt aside and stepped through the hole to see if he had stopped the demon in time.

No! He *had* to have done stopped it in time. There was simply no other outcome possible. He steeled himself and took in the scene.

Logan hovered a few feet from the demon's pointy nose, his face tight with fear and focus. Red hair bobbed behind a pile of rocks. Relief flooded through Matthias's body and almost lost him his footing.

Thank God. Both alive.

But not if they stayed here.

"Shove off!" Matthias told them. "This nasty bugger is mine!"

The demon lurched and nearly jerked him off his feet. Again. It most definitely dislodged most of his fear and left some room for common sense.

He flashed Logan a smile. "On second thought, mate, maybe you could give me a hand getting him back to the portal."

Logan dropped to his feet and said, "Stay back."

Tethered to the demon, Matthias couldn't much move, but he leaned back to steady the ropes. Logan rolled his shoulders, then brought his bow and arrow up and took the shot.

The arrow pinged off the wall.

Matthias blinked and did a double-take. Logan *missed?* Logan *never* missed.

Then the arrow ricocheted back toward the demon, and instead of piercing flesh, it arced around the monster in a spiraling rotation down the long body. It created a whirlwind, encapsulating the squirming hellion and lifting it off the ground, swaddled like a babe in the eye of Logan's tornado.

Well. Son of a gun. The cheeky sod was getting creative.

The arrow made one final pass to swirl once around Matthias. It ruffled his sweaty hair before evaporating into wisps of pearly smoke.

Yep. Cheeky, creative, and downright sassy.

He didn't want to laugh in case Logan thought he was making fun of him. So he concentrated on giving his whips a tug. Much to his relief, the demon didn't resist, but instead glided closer. He yanked harder and dragged the demon back through the hole, the creature literally floating on air.

He gave Logan an appreciative smile. "That's new. Something you been working on?"

"Well, you know, just trying to, uh, change things up." Logan followed after him, readjusting his battered suit coat.

"I like it," Matthias said.

Look at that. Captured the demon, and managed to save Logan *and* Aurora from the "robots." Speaking of...

Matthias slid a quick glance behind him. Aurora still hid behind the rocks.

He turned to Logan, fighting to keep a grin off his face. "So where did you and the nitwit come from?"

That brought Aurora jumping to her feet, any fear quickly replaced by a sneer. Matthias smirked back.

Logan shook his head. "Craziest thing..."

FAN INTERVIEW

Ayden, Jayden, Logan, Tristan, and Aurora shift uncomfortably on stage and glance nervously at two empty chairs. Matthias stomps in.

Logan: Find him?

Matthias: Nope. *drags spare chair to opposite side of row*

Tristan: What are you doing?

Matthias: Like I'm going sit through an interview next to *that.*

Aurora: *sticks tongue out* I wanted Blake to sit next to me anyway.

Matthias: *pointedly looks around* He's not here so guess he found out where he was sitting and decided not to show.

Blake: Sorry, I'm late. Had to pick something up. *bursts in waving bouquet of flowers* Show me my interviewing goddess! My soulmate, my— *sees the crowd of ladies there to ask Hex Boy questions* That, uh, wow, that is more than one lady. *glances down at bouquet* Definitely not enough.

Logan: Sit down!

Claudia: Blake, can you relate your first kiss?

HEX BOYS: No.

Blake: Aw come on—

Logan: No.

Blake: But—

Tristan: Nooo.

Blake: These girls would—

Ayden: We made a pact.

Blake: Look how sad Claudia is! We can't let her down.

Jayden: The contract was binding.

Blake: Yeah, but we made that back when we were only—

Matthias: Still stands.

Aurora: *looks around at all the Hex Boys* Your Bro Code is frightening.

Cierra: Alright fellas, who would you rather go out on a date with, Aurora or someone on your team?

Blake: Aurora, duh.

Ayden: You can't date my girlfriend.

Jayden: Technically—

Blake: Relax dude, it's all hypothermial. *winks at Aurora and whispers,* Think he bought it?

Aurora: You do know we're *not* dating, right?

Blake: Sure, chickadee, sure. *winks again*

Aurora: *sighs*

Jayden: I'm uncertain who I would chose. Aurora would seem the obvious choice as I would be able to practice dating with a female, but opposites do attract so perhaps I should choose Blake.

Blake: Boom! Another one for Team Blake!

Jayden: He's whimsical, spontaneous, and socially adept. Qualities I would need in a partner to compensate for my deficiency in those areas. I could also use the date as a means to learn from him how to attract the opposite sex. All the females love him.

HEX BOYS: No, they don't.

Blake: Jealous much?

Jayden: But, even still, I think Tristan would be the best date.

Tristan: *freezes* What?

Jayden: Our recreational and intellectual pursuits are quite compatible. Since we have plenty to bond over, we would have the most enjoyable time.

Tristan: *frowns* Actually…yeah, we would. I'd chose Jayden. Video game marathon and pizza.

Jayden: *smiles* I'd bake you cookies.

Blake: But what about our attraction! You never gave our love a chance!

Jayden: But we never actually—

Logan: I'd choose Blake.

Blake: Aw, yeah! *fist pumps air*

Aurora: *leans towards Cierra and whispers* Is it weird that I'm getting a little offended that no one is choosing me?

Logan: We always hang out. It wouldn't be any different.

Blake: *scoffs* If it was date it would be! You'd have to open the door, get me flowers. Give me compliments. The restaurant better be good and—

Logan: Never mind. I pick Aurora.

Blake: What?! No take-backs!

Aurora: Yes take-backs!

Blake: Then he's missing out.

Aurora: *Hooks arm around Logan's neck* Please, our date would be way better than yours.

Ayden: *points to self* Boyfriend sitting right here. Boyfriend who would pick you first over a date with any of his teammates.

Tristan: Matthias, who would you choose?

Matthias: Anyone but Aurora.

Aurora: Shocker.

Ayden: *smirks* I don't know why you keep pretending you aren't in love with her.

Matthias: *glares and then the lights flicker*

Blake: You'd chose me, right?

Ayden: Oh please, he'd chose Tristan.

Matthias: I'd chose Logan.

Logan: *squeaks*

Matthias: *points at a Hex Boy as he says their name* Tristan would tell me everything he's worried about. My head would hurt from translating Jayden all night. Blake talks too much about himself.

Blake: What's wrong with that?

Matthias: Ayden talks too much about Aurora.

Ayden: *winks at Aurora* What's wrong with that?

Aurora: *smiles*

Matthias: Ugh. See what I mean? So the choice is easy. Logan. He's quiet.

Jayden: *chuckles*

Ayden: You realize he insulted you too.

Jayden: Affirmative, but even with my plethora of idiosyncratic qualities—

Ayden: Translation – annoying qualities.

Jayden: I got picked to be a date, *me,* but no one picked you.

Ayden: *rolls his eyes* Like I want to spend more time with any of you guys? And on a date? Please. Besides, the only one I want to choose me is—

Aurora: Me. *hugs Ayden* I'd pick you every time.

Ayden: *smirks at Jayden* Yeah. Lucky you. I'm devastated.

Emily: What was the first thought you had when you met Aurora?

Tristan: Loud.

Aurora: I wasn't that loud.

Tristan: Your family was. So were you. All the shouting. You kept forgetting Oron in one of the empty moving boxes.

Aurora: It wasn't me *every* time.

Tristan: But you wouldn't talk to me so—

Aurora: *I* wouldn't talk to *you?*

Tristan: You did the neighborly head nod and not much else. Shy, quiet, only came outside for the evening run. You being a vampire crossed my mind—

Aurora: Wait, are vampires real?

Tristan: —but I was just happy you kept to yourself.

Matthias: If only it had stayed that way.

Blake: I thought "Oh no, damsel in distress!" because babe ran into me. I was worried she was hurt because, you know, I'm rock solid. Get it? *Rock* sol—

Logan: They get it.

Blake: And I thought babe was a total babe. I mean, who wouldn't. I told her I'd be the X on her treasure map, and I was right, wasn't I Logan?

Logan: Not exactly. Ah, my first thought was that something was off. Tristan and Ayden had just told us about the demon attack and Aurora was acting suspicious at P.E.

Aurora: Suspicious how?

Logan: Oh, um, *straightens jacket cuffs* Normal new kid stuff. But I realized that I thought you were off because you were familiar, that somehow I knew you.

Blake: Felt the same way.

HEX BOYS: No you didn't!

Jayden: My first thought was that she might be mentally incompetent. Her movements were slow and uncoordinated.

Aurora: Because Tristan had just whammied me!

Matthias: *mutters* Not hard enough.

Tristan: *points at Aurora* Still sorry about that. *points at Matthias* And you should be too. If you hadn't—

Matthias: Whatever. My first thought she was trouble. Nothing but trouble. And look how right I was. And my second thought was "Unfortunately, there are too many witnesses."

Aurora: Hardy-har-har. You're just lucky I didn't take you down that first day in the cafeteria.

Matthias: *laughs* I wish you had tried. Oh, wait. You did. And, oh look at me, I'm still here.

Aurora: I'd rather never look at you again at all.

Ayden: *turns Aurora away from Matthias* Good idea.

Jayden: Since Matthias interrupted my succession of thoughts, I will express my second observation that she was *much* larger and heavier than Blake had led me to believe.

Aurora: *squints with irritation*

Ayden: *sighs* Great.

Blake: *shakes head* Dude.

Jayden: I think people often underestimate the actual weight of a human body. And a female Aurora's immense size—

Aurora: Was the "immense" really necessary?

Matthias: *smiles* Oh yeah.

Jayden: It's an appropriate adjective to illustrate the difficulty of carrying one your significantly measurable weight.

Ayden: *rolls eyes* That did not sound better.

Jayden: *looks around confused* My observation is fact based, not related to merit. Aurora is taller than the average female, and now that I am discerning the situation more clearly, I must conclude that with our training, her muscle mass has increased considerably. So the probability has increased that she actually weighs more now. Aurora, perhaps you could share how much weight you have gained since meeting us?

Tristan: Next! Next! Who hasn't gone?

Ayden: I'll take it. I thought she was going to die the first time I saw her and I was totally wrong. First thoughts can be so stupid, absurd, insensitive, moronic, blockheaded—

Jayden: I feel like this is somehow about me.

Ayden: Oh, sure, *that* he picks up on.

Blake: Hey, Ayden, what was your second thought about Aurora?

Ayden: Ah... I thought, "Wow, she's fast."

Tristan: *snorts* That wasn't your second thought.

Ayden: *smirks* Maybe it was my third.

Tristan: *chuckling*

Jayden: But your statement coincides with the events that transpired. Aurora was being attacked by a demon and you subsequently subdued her while she ran.

Blake: And she is fast. Babe, when you run, you sweat in a totally sexy way. Your shirt clings to— *gasps and points at Ayden* I know your real second thought! You tackled her! Got a look down her—

Logan: Blake!

Ayden: He's not wrong.

Aurora: Really?

Ayden: Oh. Ah. Well, I did admit that I can find certain parts of your anatomy mesmerizing. *rubs back of neck* But what I must be talking about is the demon. I got a real good look at the demon, because I'm a gentleman.

Aurora: *tries to frown but ends up laughing* Alright, someone want to save Ayden with a change of topic?

Anna: What are Ayden's thoughts on Cristiano?

Aurora: *ignores Anna and scans crowd* Anyone? Anyone at all have a nice question that's not a sore spot for any of the Hex Boys?

Anna: #TeamCristiano

Aurora: *facepalms* Way to save the day, Anna.

Ayden: Cacciatori, eh? Sure. He's—

Blake: Sexy.

Ayden: Thanks Blake. You'd know better than I since you offered to have him kiss you.

Blake: I didn't offer. I just said I wouldn't mind. Big difference.

Ayden: *smirks* Sure it is. So... *heavy sigh* Well, I'd like to know more about him, like what his power is, what his true intentions are. About all we do know is that he and his entire

Sicarius team are ruthless. And the truth is, I'm grateful he showed up.

Aurora: Really?

HEX BOYS: *give him doubtful looks*

Ayden: He protected Aurora when we couldn't. Plus he saved Blake.

Blake: Aw. Thanks dude. I wouldn't mind if you kiss me either.

Ayden: *shudders* I would.

Aurora: Me too. *kisses Ayden's cheek* Alright, let's try an easy question this time ladies!

Emily: Only one, so hard to choose. Can any of you pinpoint where Fleur-De-Lys is on a world map?

Aurora: Emily, we have very different definitions of easy.

Emily: I'll give you two hints, it isn't in the US and it isn't a national park.

HEX BOYS: *glance confused amongst each other then all look at one Hex Boy*

Jayden: Why are you all looking at me?

Blake: Dude, if anyone knows, it's you.

Jayden: Why me? You are earth.

Tristan: Mediterranean Sea between Italy and Libya? Malta?

HEX BOYS: *stare stunned*

Aurora: *also stunned*

Tristan: *holds up smart phone* Internet. So, I guess the answer to your question is "No." Sorry, Emily. But points for stumping even genius Jayden.

Blake: I bet Cristiano knows where it is. He knows everything.

Logan: Abort the Cristiano talk.

Blake: But he's my hero!

Emily: If you could trade powers with anyone else on the team, who would it be and why?

Jayden: I would trade with Tristan. It would be fascinating to truly understand how people think and feel.

Ayden: I'd take Blake's.

Blake: Won't make you as awesome as me, but it'd be an improvement.

Ayden: *ignoring the big guy* It'd be nice to create for once instead of destroy.

Logan: I'd, uh, I'd choose fire.

Jayden: Really?

Blake: Duh.

Jayden: *huffs* It's hardly the obvious choice.

Blake: Do you know how much concentration it takes to make a breeze deadly?

Logan: *nods* It would be nice to have a power that's easily weaponized. Less tiring.

Tristan: I'd take Matthias's for the opposite reason. His power would deal the least amount of damage if I lost control.

Matthias: Wouldn't be so sure about that mate.

Blake: *pitches voice shrill* Oh no, it's dark! Whatever will I do! It's not like I deal with the dark every night!

Logan: *smacks Blake*

Matthias: *raises hand and shadows wrap around Blake until there's a helmet of solid, fathomless black surrounding his head*

Blake: *voice muffled* Only people you're scaring are the ladies, depriving them of all of this. *Waves hand in front of where his face would be*

Matthias: *rolls eyes and releases shadows* What power would you take then, moron?

Blake: *blinks at brightness* Pssh, wouldn't trade my powers for anything.

Ayden: It's hypothetical.

Blake: I don't care if it's cold.

HEX BOYS: *sigh*

Blake: Alright, if I *had* to. I'd take Logan's. Flying would be sweet. What about you, dude?

Matthias: Tristan's.

Aurora: What a surprise. The control-freak wants the power that could brainwash us into doing what he wants.

Matthias: …Sure.

Jayden: *gasps* No one wants my power?!

Ayden: You got picked for a date.

Jayden: Yes, but by Tristan.

Tristan: What's that supposed to mean?!

Esther: How do you keep the extension of your powers a secret from the Mandatum? Especially when you were younger?

Matthias: Blake! You told them! How many times have I told you to keep your bloody mouth shut!

Blake: It wasn't me!

Jayden: Our parents helped us conceal our abilities.

Matthias: Jayden!

Jayden: There's nothing to be ashamed of. We were ten. No one would expect us to be able to conceal ourselves from a conglomerate the immense power of the Mandatum at that age. And now that we are capable, we do most of the falsifying on our own.

Matthias: *groans*

Ayden: But mostly it's like getting a few problems wrong so that you aren't bumped up into advanced Calculus in your freshmen year.

Logan: Or throwing a game when you know you could make every shot.

Esther: Did you have a problem with killing demons at the beginning of your training?

Logan: No.

Blake: I thought I would but once there's a demon in front of you it's do or die. They come flying at you!

Jayden: The Mandatum makes certain they unleash the most irate demons upon the trainees.

Blake: Oh yeah. *loses enthusiasm and frowns* Remember that one girl on the other team?

Tristan: Hard to forget that much blood.

Ayden: I didn't have a problem. I saw one of my best friends, Garret, get ripped to shreds. Taking down the demons felt like a way to honor him. And truth is, I didn't want to end up in the same boat.

Tristan: Me neither. But at least you could turn demons to ash. I just kept making it think I wasn't there and tricking it into running into things while I tried to run away but the teacher wouldn't let me—

Matthias: I'm sure the ladies don't want to be bored with the details of our training.

Aurora: Yeeeaaah *turns wide eyes away from boys* Yeah, sure, new *fun* question.

Cierra: Jayden, have you ever been to Kauai?

Aurora: Perfect.

Cierra: It's the wettest place on Earth, and I'm wondering if you know that and if you've been there, if you've ever done anything with your abilities? ^-^

Jayden: Yes, I have. My mother is actually from Hawaii.

Ayden: We'd vacation in Kauai to practice our powers. Plenty of water for him and not as easy for me to burn everything down.

Jayden: So that would be a yes I *did* know that it is the wettest place on earth. And I experimented with my powers at great length there.

Blake: Kayaked up a waterfall.

Jayden: *smiles* Ah. One of my favorite memories. It was Jocelyn's idea. That necessitated Tristan accompanying us on our travels. Back then I wasn't very good looking out for witnesses before I dabbled in childish antics.

Tristan: You still aren't. You let those guys from school see you shut down Ayden's fire when we were in the restaurant parking lot.

Jayden: That was because of Ayden's childish behavior.

Ayden: Hey!

Matthias: Let's agree to disagree...with Ayden and agree with Jayden and move on.

Ayden: Very funny.

Matthias: I am the comedian of the group.

Cierra: Aurora! You know that accented voice you hear in your head? Is it an Italian accent....or an Australian one? 3:)

Aurora: *squints at Cierra* Gee thanks.

Ayden: What voice in your head?

Aurora: Not in my head. There are voices in my dreams. Like everybody has.

Ayden: A guy's voice?

Aurora: I don't have control over my dreams. Do you?

Blake: She's dodging the question! She's totally dreaming about me! What are we doing?

Aurora: Nothing because it's not you. It's not anybody. I don't see him. I can barely hear him so—

Blake: It could still totally be me.

Logan: You don't have an accent.

Jayden: Of course he does. It's American.

Tristan: But she wouldn't describe our own accent as an accent.

Jayden: But our accent is an accent so—

Aurora: Look, I don't know what accent the dream guy has. He speaks too low and the dreams are all fuzzy. Like most dreams. Could be Southern or Swahili for all I know. It really doesn't matter.

Matthias: It better not be an Australian accent.

Aurora: *taps chin thoughtfully* Actually, now that you mention it, maybe the accent was Australian.

Matthias: *shudders*

Aurora: Relax, the only time your voice pops up is in my nightmares.

Matthias: I'd prefer you didn't dream of me at all, but nightmares are okay.

Cierra: Aurora, let's play 'Kiss Marry Kill' with two groups. First up - Ayden, Jayden, Blake.

Blake: Sorry, Fireboy. *puts hand on Aurora's shoulder* Let him down easy, babe.

Aurora: *smirks* Kiss Jayden, marry Ayden, kill Blake.

Blake: WHAT?

Aurora: I can't kill my husband's brother.

Blake: But you can kill *me?*

Jayden: Excellent choice, Aurora. Would there be tongues involved in our kiss? What are the rules to this game? I do not think it should count unless there are tongues.

Ayden: Never mind, you can kill Jayden.

Blake: I'm back in the game! Come on, babe! *leans down and puckers lips*

Aurora: *rolls eyes*

Ayden: *shoves Blake away*

Cierra: Okay, second group – Tristan, Matthias, Logan.

Tristan: I think we can all guess who's getting killed in the next round.

Aurora: I'd kiss Matthias.

HEX BOYS: WHAT?

Ayden: Are you serious?

Matthias: Please say no.

Jayden: And once again, there must be tongues.

Matthias: Please, *please* say no.

Aurora: Oh yeah. I am perfectly serious. He'd die from me kissing him.

Matthias: *grimacing* She's not wrong, mates.

Aurora: If I kill Tristan, then his grandparents will kill me in a slow and tortuous death.

Tristan: Not wrong there either.

Aurora: Right? Your grandma already had me in a body bag.

Ayden: *On* the body bag.

Aurora: Point is, it's got my name on it. So I marry Tristan, gaining their protection, and Logan is saved because I both kissed and killed Matthias. *points at Logan* You're welcome.

Blake: You save Logan, but not me?! And why does Matthias get tongue but I didn't?

Matthias: Just kill me now.

Aurora: Pucker up, lover boy.

Matthias: *closes eyes and gags*

Cierra: Blake, what is your favorite flower?

Everyone but Blake groans

Ayden: Don't get him started.

Blake: Started? I never stop!

Matthias: True enough.

Blake: I *might* have I've mentioned the Passiflora before. I love it because it's very much like each of you gorgeous ladies. Unique, passionate, and it holds the fruit of love.

Tristan: You always love to work that in.

Blake: The work of adoring of the ladies is never done.

Logan: Unfortunately.

Blake: But my favorite is the kadupul flower. It only blooms at midnight and its gone by dawn. I always wanted to take a girl out to see. Out under the stars, the perfume of the blooms filling the air, admiring its fleeting beauty—

Jayden: I thought that was your second favorite flower.

Blake: Shhh!

Logan: His favorite is the Chocolate Cosmos. It's really rare and smells like chocolate.

Blake: Dude!

Logan: Girls like chocolate.

Aurora: We do.

Blake: Good point. And they do both smell good… and are almost as pretty as you ladies!

Tristan: Ugh, give it a rest.

Cierra: Logan how would you ask someone out?

Logan: I wouldn't.

Blake: I'd do it for you.

HEX BOYS: No!

Jayden: I would be a much more effective proxy for your dating extravaganza. I would say, "Excuse me, potential female mate, Logan finds your secretion of pheromones to be hormonally arousing and—"

HEX BOYS: No!

Logan: That's worse.

Aurora: *Secretions? *whispers to other Hex Boys** How did he not fail the seduction course?

Logan: I'd put a note in her locker.

Tristan: Classic. And a very safe approach.

Blake: Jayden, maybe you should give Cristiano a call. Run some dating ideas by him. Or I could ask him for you. We talk all time.

Matthias: Since when?

Blake: He hasn't returned my calls yet. But when he does—

Matthias: Hell will see a snow storm.

Blake: Awesome! We could go sledding. Aurora can get us there. It's on the way to the Waiting World, right?

Gwen: Aurora, is it hard to be around so many boys?

Aurora: They're an improvement on Lucian. They're more mature, but not by much.

Blake: Hey! I'm way more mature than Lucian. Just look at my glutes! *turns around, lifts his flannel shirt and points at his backside* Just watch me torque them! I can do it to music. Pick a song!

HEX BOYS: *all jump in front of him to block the view*

Ayden: Not again.

Tristan: He always finds a way.

Matthias: Bloody hell.

Aurora: *laughs* They're certainly entertaining. Plus, I'm used to the crazy with my own family, and it's nice to be around people I can trust and be honest with.

Ayden: *snorts*

Matthias: *snorts*

Tristan: *snorts*

Aurora: *huffs* Well I'm honest *now*. Not like you guys made it easy. Especially you, Aussie man.

Matthias: Why would I make it easy? I didn't want you anywhere near us. Still don't.

Aurora: And as for needing girl time—

Blake: She can always come to me about girl stuff. Mascara, tampons, I know it all.

HEX BOYS: *cringe*

Aurora: I've got Katie, Natasha, and Mika at school. And Luna's always around whether I want her to be or not. But no, I don't find it hard. I love spending time with these guys.

Matthias: Maybe you should spend less time with us.

Aurora: *eyes Matthias* Well, love spending time with *most* of them.

Matthias: I'm crushed.

Aurora: Ready for that kiss yet? With tongue?

Matthias: *groans*

Maria: What exactly is Aurora's "explody power?" It's electrified in some way as when Aurora is thrown off the cliff, her hands spark on Matthias but if she were in water, would she had electrocuted herself and others? Does her power work on herself? Her teleportation ability is mental isn't it? It's her "safeguard." The guys got bubbles when they were attacked but Aurora is actually transported to another place–another (dimension? Plane?) realm.

Aurora: *smiles, snaps fingers and points at Maria* I've got no idea. But I love that you think I do. Thanks!

Jayden: Logan and I have been probing these inquiries ourselves.

Ayden: Because the rest of us never sit around worrying about it.

Jayden: Also, why does it grant her immunity to some powers but not others? Immune to Tristan and the Sheriff, but Blake could crush her under a boulder. Actually, we haven't tried that.*stands up* Blake, Aurora, let's go outside and—

Ayden: *yanks his brother down* Don't you dare. Putting that brain contraption on her head was bad enough. Gave her a headache for a week. Not to mention the nightmares.

Aurora: How did you know about those?

Ayden: I know a bit more than you get me credit for.

Maria: Does anyone in Aurora's family have powers?

Aurora: God I hope not.

Logan: If they had powers, they could protect themselves from demons.

Aurora: Oh, hadn't thought of that. God I hope so.

Jayden: We have been over this. The Divinicus does not come from a Mandatum bloodline, therefore, there is no hunter power your parents could have or pass on to your siblings.

Aurora: Divinicus isn't supposed to be a girl either so...

Jayden: We thoroughly investigated your family!

Aurora: *sighs* I know.

Jayden: Weeks and weeks!

Ayden: Yes, Jayden, we get it. Relax.

Maria: Will we ever meet Aurora's grandmother? ...the (elf/fairy) slayer?

Aurora: Ideally, no. Not a great time for the family to come visiting, me being a supernatural danger magnet and all. Although I do miss her and Grandpa.

Salaria: Matthias can you kiss Aurora? Please and thank you.

Matthias: No! What is wrong with you?

Ayden: *chuckles* That I would like to see. You have my full support...mate. Go for it.

Blake: Another team challenge? Okay, Matthias, but I'm still number one.

Aurora: Relax, I'm going to end Team Matthias with a kiss, remember?

Matthias: Could you just stab me instead?

Evelyn: Jayden, what qualities are you looking for when you find a girlfriend?

Jayden: My idea mate would be—

Ayden: A computer.

Tristan: An A.I.

Matthias: Non-existent.

Jayden: **glares** I have made it quite clear that I am not completely sapiosexual.

Logan: **gulps** Oh, God. What did he just say?

Ayden: **blinks** I have no clue.

Blake: **grins** I hope it means—

Matthias: Shut it, mate. No one wants to hear what you think it means.

Jayden: It means that my ideal mate would not necessarily have to be my intellectual equal. I place a much higher value on patience and social skills.

Blake: That's right. You wanted a girl version of Ayden.

Jayden: **cringes** I never said that.

Ayden: You don't have to sound so offended by it.

Jayden: I want a mate who could help me relate to others—

Blake: Like Ayden does.

Jayden:—and has a lust for learning... As well as lustful inclinations towards me. **winks**

Aurora: It's so cute when he's trying to be sexy.

Evelyn: What is the worst situation you can imagine while on a date?

Ayden: Getting stuck in a long conversation with a priest while some guy kidnaps your date.

Matthias: **snickers**

Tristan: My grandparents showing up and giving me pointers.

Blake: The girl doesn't laugh at my jokes.

Jayden: She doesn't understand me and Ayden's not close enough to translate.

Logan: These guys showing up.

Blake: Hey!

Ayden: He makes a good point. You guys suck.

Matthias: Not as much as a demon showing up.

Ayden: Not as bad as you'd think.

Michelle: Hey, Jayden! I'm interested if you had to choose a career, what would it be?

Jayden: *rubs chin* Hmmm. I've always found it satisfying to invent things and solve puzzles.

Tristan: Remember when he kept seeing how fast he could put together the rubik's cubic, and we all had to time him.

Logan: And then he kept trying to get us to challenge him so he could gloat about how much faster he was than any of us.

Jayden: I did not gloat. I simply found it pleasurable to point out how my speed was far superior in success than yours.

Tristan: Yes, genius. That is definitely not gloating.

Ayden: He wouldn't shut up about it. At least the rest of you didn't have to live with him.

Jayden: Regardless, when I was younger I always wanted to play with animals in the ocean. Dolphins and orcas especially. Those species are incredibly intelligent. So perhaps I would be a marine biologist.

Emily: Tell me, oh moody one. What is it that annoys you so much about Aurora?

Blake: Ayden, take it away.

Ayden: What? Emily isn't talking about me!

Blake: Oh, Logan, go ahead.

Logan: *face-palm*

Matthias: Do you have a month? The list is a mile long.

Aurora: Ahhh. I thought it was going to be two miles. I knew you liked me.

Matthias: *rolls eyes* She lies. Constantly.

Aurora: Not to you.

Matthias: *raises eyebrows*

Aurora: *Anymore.*

Matthias: She's got my team lying, keeping secrets from each other.

Aurora: Do not!

Jayden: Well, actually—

Aurora: Don't you have a fish to research?!

Matthias: She never thinks anything through, gets into trouble and expects us to bail her out. And me? I'm fine leaving her to face the consequences on her own but these idiots have to go save the damsel—

Aurora: *Damsel?*

Matthias: And get themselves killed in the process. I mean, assassins? Spies? Demon armies? Everything was fine before she showed up.

Aurora: Oh yeah, real great working for a corrupt secret society filled with more moles than whack-a-mole game. Isn't it your *job* to deal with that kind of crap anyway?

Matthias: Isn't it your *job* to keep that kind of crap from happening in the first place?

Aurora: In that case, isn't it your job to take orders from me?

Ayden: *looks at empty wrist* Oh wow, look at the time. Aurora and I are going to miss our reservation if we don't get moving. *throws Aurora over shoulder and heads out the door* Great chat, ladies. Can't wait to do this again

Matthias: *smirks* Look at the damsel getting saved.

Aurora: *glares through hair over her face* Only damsel getting saved is you, Aussie man! From me! Ayden, put me down!

Ayden: Not a chance.

Blake: *closely following Ayden and Aurora* Hey, remember when I had to throw Aurora over my shoulder to stop her from—

Matthias: Doing something stupid.

Blake: Right. And then she spanked me because I was a bad, bad boy.

Aurora: Are you kidding me? I never spanked you even though you asked me to!

Blake: Because I knew you wanted it. I mean, who wouldn't want to? And I'm feeling naughty again. *thrusts out hip* Want to—

Aurora: No!

Blake: Oh, I get it, Aurora. Since you're being naughty, you want me to spank yo—

Ayden: No! *slips outside*

Blake: *follows* Whoa, Fireboy, you want me so spank both of you? Didn't realize you were so kinky.

Matthias: *groans and winces a smile at the crowd* Thank you for your questions. Please forgive Blake's behavior.

Jayden: I do not believe you need apologize. The females do seem to enjoy his antics. Perhaps this would be an ideal time to imitate him and experiment my coquetry skills with the females present.

Tristan: Not sure exactly what you mean but I am sure the answer is a big "NO!" *pulls Jayden out chair*

Jayden: But they're smiling. And cheering my name. *waves to crowd*

Matthias: Logan.

Logan: *already running for the exit* I'll bring the car around.

Blake: *opens door and steps back in* I'm back! Didn't think I'd forgotten about you lovely ladies, did you?!

Logan: *tackles into Blake with a burst of wind and forces him back outside*

Blake: Ow! Dude!

Matthias: Thanks again for coming. *shoves Tristan and Jayden for exit* Go, go!

Jayden: I believe they wish me to remain. My intuitive skills in regards to reading human behavior have improved vastly.

CROWD: Jay-den! Jay-den!

Jayden: See? *stops and waves*

Tristan and **Matthias**: *push Jayden out and slam door closed behind them*

Blake: *voice muffled through the door* How did I lose to Team Jayden?!

ABOUT THE AUTHORS

This mother-daughter duo were in and out of inter-dimensional paranormal prisons until they finally quit making up cover stories for secret societies and started writing novels. The Supernatural Continuum Warlords of the Supernatural Continuum Warlordian High Command had pity upon them, and instead of having them slaughtered by the slow, tortuous flesh eating underwater, earthworm squid, they transported them into a habitationally friendly dimension called OOARCHTOHUTHLAMADILFRUMP, also known as 21st Century Earth. Due to a demon infestation in their sleepy mountain California town, and a lack of sexy Hex Boys to stop them, Alyssa and Eileen were forced to relocate to Los Angeles.

The Amazon bestseller, DEMONS AT DEADNIGHT, is book one in the DIVINICUS NEX CHRONICLES series, and the first of their exclusive re-creations of supernatural society secrets. You can uncover more paranormal, inter-dimensional classified information at:

AEKIRK.com and Facebook.com/AandEKirk.

Citizens of Earth, you are welcome.

Enjoy a sneak peek of A and E Kirk's exciting new series!

Midnight Poison

By

A&E Kirk

Paranormal Poisons Saga:

Book 1

Hello Reader!

Thanks for being here! We are soooooo excited for you to start MIDNIGHT POISON!

But first, a quick note, especially for the fabulous fans of our Bestselling DIVINICUS NEX CHRONICLES series.

MIDNIGHT POISON has some language and intense sexuality in comparison to the DN Chronicles. We think you will have a blast with this exciting new story and crazy fun characters, but we want to be clear.

You have been warned! So back away now, or strap in and go for it. Either way, we love you!

Hugs and Kisses All Around,
A & E

PS: Don't miss all the latest news and fun!
- Sign up for our Hexy Knight Newsletter at our website: AEKIRK.COM
- Follow us on FACEBOOK.COM/AandEKIRK,
See you there!

CHAPTER 1

A VIOLENT CRESCENDO OF SCREAMS slashed through the gentle harmonies of Mozart's haunting melody. Bright crimson sprayed the white ceiling of the massive party tent, the glowing chandeliers swayed upon impact. The scarlet liquid dripped off the thousands of glittering crystals. Leontes stared at the droplets on the back of his hand, rested his cane against the round table, and then licked away the blood.

Silence hushed through the space around him. The large crowd of rich, beautiful, powerful—and soon-to-be-dead—people attending the charity ball looked around with curiosity. Many of those sitting at the tables rose to their feet. Dancers paused their steps.

A rumble from above brought all eyes upward. The center-most chandelier trembled as shadows snaked over the white ceiling. Black vines serrated with sharp thorns ripped through the fabric. Twisting like serpents, the thick vines hissed against the material before they coiled around the chandelier. As the crystals trembled and clinked, deep red flower petals fluttered down over the crowd.

Something hit the table with a wet slap, toppling the floral centerpiece with a crash and speckling moisture onto Leontes' cheek. The human heart, so recently removed from its owner, gave one final pathetic pump and then lay limp. Black blood oozed like foul-smelling wine over the white tablecloth. The woman sitting beside Leontes gasped and clutched his hand. The others at the table choked on screams of shock.

When a slow laugh wound through the air like wind chimes on an ocean breeze, chills erupted down Leontes' spine.

"No," he whispered.

The vines strangling the chandelier burst with blooms of large black flowers.

Several partygoers shrieked in horror. "Oleander!"

A group of men ran, tossing aside tables, chairs, and each other. Anything standing between themselves and escape. More blossoms burst to life. They overflowed around the remaining chandeliers and smothered the glowing bulbs. Light faded into darkness and fueled the rising terror.

Snatching his cane, Leontes rose and took the hand of the woman sitting beside him. The stench of soured blood and eviscerated organs surged through the air. His feet slipped on something wet as he backed toward the exit. He looked down at the dark pool growing larger by the second. The woman screamed and pointed over his shoulder.

Leontes turned. He barely registered the flash of metal before his head fell from his shoulders. It hit the ground with a wet *thud*. A moment later the cane clattered beside it as the vicious sounds of the massacre echoed to nothing.

CHAPTER 2

FOR LEONTES, EVERYTHING BECAME STARTLINGLY BLACK.
No emotion or power in the abyss of nothingness. He could not
remember a time death had not ended like this. He took a deep breath
and slipped from the void. Faint light called to him. Shapes pushed
through and took on substance and color. He rubbed his neck, head
still firmly attached.

Always a comfort.

He shook his head and broke free from the vision of the past.
With another deep breath, he focused on the world around him. The
present.

Police officers and technicians hurried about in a professionally
panicked manner through the wreckage. Overturned furniture.
Broken china. Scattered food. The remnants of what had been a four-
foot-tall swan ice sculpture now lay melted on the ground. White
curtains, ripped and bloody, draped in elegant arcs around the open-
air tent big enough to house a circus.

Or in this case, a slaughter.

The wood dance floor gleamed slick with smeared blood, like a
macabre modern art piece. Strings of miniature lights hung in a
broken, haphazard mess. Several spit sparks.

Outside the tent, floodlights illuminated the expansive green lawn rolling up to a stately mansion. Littered with dozens of misshapen forms hidden beneath body sheets, the grass looked like a blizzard had dropped masses of snow in its wake.

Leontes flexed his fingers around the cane in his hand. He could still feel the pull of the memories attached to it. The endless loop of someone else's pain and fear yearned to yank him in to relive it all, again and again, but his centuries of experience made him more than able to resist. He knelt and set the cane on the blood-soaked sheet that covered what remained of the cane's owner.

He pulled a pair of black leather gloves from his coat and slipped them on. He had touched enough of the various victims' items to piece together what had happened here.

A middle-aged, mustached detective in a cheap sports coat and latex gloves entered the tent and gazed around.

"Looks like one hell of a party. Get it? *Hell* of a party." He chuckled.

Leontes did not laugh.

He stood tall, lean, and muscular, an imposing figure in a black trench coat over an expertly tailored Italian three-piece suit. He looked to be in his mid-twenties, with handsome, aristocratic features finely formed from generations of good breeding. But there was nothing soft about him.

Under high cheekbones, a perpetual five o'clock shadow covered his square jaw and surrounded full lips which were currently tipped into a frown. His cobalt blue eyes held a hard look that demanded respect. Against dark waves of hair that curled softly at the ends, his skin had always been pale, but more so now, which made the thin scar across his neck stand out even in this dim light.

From his vest, he removed a gold pocket watch hanging on a chain and opened it briefly. Dawn was several hours away, but with a mess of this magnitude they would still have to move fast. Leontes scanned the room, rolling his shoulders to shake off the shadows of the recent past and concentrate on the present.

He spoke with a strong British accent, his noble heritage evident in the tone and cadence. "Have you any relevant information as of yet?"

"Look, kid." The officer puffed out his chest. "I'm Detective Cage. This is a crime scene. Authorized personnel only. You can't be here. I'm going to have to ask you to leave immediately." He waved his hand in a gesture of dismissal.

Leontes held up his credentials.

"Holy shit," the detective muttered.

Not bothering to look at the man, Leontes strode past and spoke in a lecturing tone, "Language, detective. Language."

Cage's chest deflated. "Oh, yeah. I mean, uh, yes, sir. Sorry, um, Ambassador Rittenhause, sir. I didn't mean to…I didn't recognize you. Sir."

Leontes looked the man up and down. "I do not recall us having met."

Detective Cage bobbed his head. "No, sir, we haven't, but—"

"Then, *detective*, how would you expect to recognize me?"

The man squirmed. "I guess I wouldn't. But I know your reputation. Sir. Sorry you have to see this."

See this? If he only knew. "I am sorry anyone has to see this."

"Yeah, but sorry about all the blood and bodies and stuff. Messy. I know you don't like that kind of thing."

Leontes lifted a brow. "Do you now?"

"Well, uh, that's the word." Cage swallowed. "You being a diplomat and all. Like I said, I know your reputa—"

"Indeed. Whoever was in charge previously, go inform them this scene is now mine."

Leontes lifted the nearest sheet, beneath lay what used to be a torso. Someone had shattered the sternum and hinged the chest open at the spine. Ribs hung with wet strings of flesh. The lungs and ropes of intestines sat inside like the tongue of a clam. The neck was a pulpy stump. With the hips ripped off, there was no confirmation of the gender, but the size of the shoulders tended toward male.

"If they sent you, it must be true." The detective's voice lowered. "Oleander is back."

Leontes dropped the sheet. "Oleander died centuries ago."

Detective Cage smirked. "So did we."

Leontes shot him an annoyed glance that stuttered the smirk into submission, then he flicked the tail of his coat back and knelt to lift up a new sheet. Heavily muscled arm. Deep, oozing lacerations. The round tip of the humorous bone jutted out, ready to be popped back into a shoulder that was likely scattered under another sheet. In the midst of all this, finding that shoulder could prove difficult.

"How many victims?" Leontes asked.

"We don't know. A hundred, two hundred? Can't be sure until we piece bodies back together. You were alive back when Oleander was loose, right?"

Leontes stood. "Have you not found the guest list?"

"Guest list?"

"Security was excruciatingly tight. You had to be on a list to be allowed entrance."

"You would know," Detective Cage said with not-so-subtle envy. "I'll have someone look for that."

Idiot. Leontes pinched the bridge of his nose and took a deep breath. "Start your search with the dead security guards out front."

Detective Cage started to turn away, but stopped. "They say Oleander is feral. A machine with one goal. Destroy everything. How did you stay alive? How do we all stay alive?"

Before he could answer, a female voice said, "By not jumping to conclusions, you fopdoodle."

CHAPTER 3

LEONTES SMILED.

All four-feet-eight-inches of Dr. Victoria Frankenstein stomped in wearing dainty boots that glistened with blood and dew. Revered for her brilliant scientific mind, she had been utilized by vampire masters for centuries. Many considered sunscreen to be among her greatest inventions. It poured billions in revenue into their coffers when sold to the humans and allowed vampires to live 'outside the box,' as the in-house marketing slogan stated. Most importantly, it solidified her spot in the vampire hierarchy.

"Good evening, Frankie," Leontes said evenly.

With a fierce glare on her face, Frankie tugged a hot pink cardigan over her small shoulders and smoothed her hands over the slim skirt of her black dress. She wore bright green, cat's-eye glasses on a face full of rounded features, her thin lips currently set in a frown. She tucked back a few blonde strands of hair that had dared to escape the tightly wrapped bun at the nape of her head.

Normally, Leontes was happy to see her. Normally, she was not shooting him dirty looks. So he was grateful when her ferocious fawn-brown eyes turned on the detective. Leontes may have intimidated him, but the detective visibly withered as he stared down the wrath of the tiny woman's bespectacled glare.

"This is brutal, yes," Frankie snapped in a voice that tremored with a vague accent of old European. She stepped close to the detective and craned her neck up to address him, continuing her rant, but then scowled and looked around.

Without a word, Leontes righted a folding chair and offered his hand. She took it and let him help her step onto the seat, then gave him a stiff nod of irritated gratitude.

Using her newly found loft, Frankie glared at Cage eye to eye. "But other than flowers any idiot could plant, I see no indication that this was Oleander."

Leontes glanced at the black oleanders blooming out of the chandeliers above. He would not say *any* idiot.

"He also left the calling card," Cage said.

"Oh," Frankie said, clearly disappointed. "We still must investigate to be sure." She jumped off the chair, then put her hands on her hips and faced Leontes.

He turned away on the pretense of studying the scene once again.

"You son of a bitch," she said.

Leontes refrained from comment, but a sudden thought tightened his chest. "Where is Kiara?"

"At the mansion, locked up under the evil queen's watchful eye. Not that you'd know or care."

"Good." Leontes breathed easier, a soft sigh escaping his lips. Frankie had certainly gotten more dramatic over the last few hundred years. He knelt on one knee and removed a glove to inspect another corpse.

Frankie's booted foot connected squarely with his backside. To keep from falling, he squished a hand into the intestines of some poor bastard who had only been counting on champagne and caviar. Not evisceration.

"I'm not being dramatic," Frankie said.

Leontes flicked his hand, flinging off chunks of clotted blood and mutilated flesh. "I never said you were."

"Sure you didn't. You haven't called in over a month." She kicked him again.

The detective snorted. At Leontes' harsh look, the man quickly busied himself with a notebook and took a step back.

"I have been overseas working the Oleander case," Leontes said mildly.

"Rubbish," Frankie said.

That it was, but he would never admit it. Leontes avoided her gaze and removed a handkerchief from his pocket to clean the carnage off his hand. "I have uncovered some disturbing news regarding Kiara," he said. "We must retain a closer watch upon her. And it is imperative that we keep her confined. Why are you not at the mansion?"

"Mass murder at a party for the undead elite which our queen and *you* were supposed to attend?" Frankie sniffed. "She sent all her best."

"Where is she, by the way? Is she safe?" Leontes asked.

"She had Elliot call. That's her new limo driver, which you would know if you had bothered to keep in touch," Frankie said in a scolding tone. "They had a flat tire and now, of course, she isn't coming."

"A lucky coincidence," Leontes said, looking around. "Another vampire master died tonight."

"With the two killed last month in the Middle East and Asia, we're losing them fast," Frankie said. "Maybe the killer was planning to take the queen out as well."

"Perhaps," Leontes said. "Whoever is responsible for these killings is escalating. They hit the sorcerers hard last week in Europe. I was too late. I am always too late."

"I don't care that you didn't call me," Frankie said. "But Kiara? She asked about you every day, you know. Now it's every hour. She's unraveling without you."

Leontes gritted his teeth. "I am sure she is fine."

The detective glanced at them both. "Is that the crazy girl the queen keeps locked in the tower?"

Leontes stifled a growl. "Why are you still here?"

At Frankie's nod of confirmation, Cage continued, "Yeah, that girl is *so* not fine."

"See?" Frankie said.

Leontes glowered at the detective. "Perhaps we should focus on the serial killer. That might help prove that you have some worth to the investigation."

"Yeah," Frankie said. "Are you sure you're even a detective? Fopdoodle seems more appropriate."

Cage's cheeks reddened. "Is this about my badge going missing? I've already been reprimanded. I still say one of those pennies took it when I was at the mansion for our last monthly meeting. You know how they are. Sneaky. And useless, except for—"

With lightning speed, Leontes was upon him, wrapping the fingers of one hand around the man's throat and easily lifting him in the air. Choking, eyes bugged, the terrified detective clawed at

Leontes' hand, feet kicking but finding no purchase. He, too, had inhuman strength, but was no match for the old vampire.

Leontes snarled with fury. Cage kept struggling, but his movements slowly became weaker.

"Pipe down," Frankie said, swacking Leontes' back. "Now who's being dramatic?"

For several moments, Detective Cage's future seemed to hang in the balance. Then, with a noise of disgust, Leontes released him. Cage dropped, barely managing to stay on his feet, and grabbed at his neck.

"What the hell, man!" he croaked. "I mean, sir. But...jeez. What the hell!"

"So," Frankie said to Cage. "What has a dimwit like you so convinced this is Oleander?"

Keeping a wary eye on Leontes, the detective coughed and swallowed a few times before speaking. "The survivors. Before our ambulances took them away, they said they saw Oleander."

Cold washed over Leontes' body. *"Survivors?"*

Frankie's jaw took on a hard edge. "Oleander doesn't leave survivors."

"Well," Cage said, "these guys barely made it out with their lives."

"Call the queen." Leontes stood and raced toward his car. "Lock down the entire institute!"

"Leontes, what's going on?" Frankie called.

"The queen sent more than half of her house to investigate this!" Leontes called over his shoulder.

"Of course, but with an attack of this magnitude, how could she not send everyone?" Frankie put a hand to her mouth as realization struck. "Oh my God."

The mansion was nearly empty. Kiara was defenseless.

CHAPTER 4

"**SOMEONE IS BREAKING INTO THE MANSION,**" Butch said quietly, his tone urgent.

"Go away." Kiara buried her head under her pillow and tried to reclaim sleep.

"They're right outside your window."

Kiara lifted her head. In the filthy gloom of night, a cloaked figure swung over the railing and onto her balcony.

"It ain't a dream." The thin, old man knelt beside her bed. "Move."

Now fully awake and keeping an eye on the intruder outside, Kiara slunk off the far side of the bed and onto the stone floor. The cold quickly chilled her bare feet and reached her skin through the thin material of her nightgown.

The intruder paused outside the doors, hooded head doing a slow sweep. Kiara ducked and scanned the space, too. She had always loved her room, but now, noting it had glass walls and resided at the top of a tall tower with only one way in or out, it was not ideal.

She had worked hard to keep the space open and free of clutter, with cozy armchairs and tall armoires strategically placed around the perimeter, leaving nothing but a rug on the center of the open floor.

Plants bloomed outside on the wraparound balcony, but none were big enough for her to hide behind.

Dark, from either the middle of the night or the very early morning, the stars twinkled in and out of clouds moving across the sky. Fog rolled in off the forest behind the mansion. Kiara pondered the idea of making a run for the doors to the balcony on the other side of the room. She could jump and lose the intruder in the mist.

Kneeling beside her, Butch's watery blue eyes followed her gaze. "That's a five-story drop. Don't even think about it."

The doors squeaked softly. Kiara dropped flat. Looking from under the bed, she saw the intruder swing the balcony doors open and step inside, bringing with him the sound of crashing surf and the salty aroma of the ocean. The rush of fresh air fanned the fire in the hearth, renewing life into flames, which had dwindled low.

Butch scowled at her. "You didn't lock the doors?"

"It's a five-story climb," Kiara hissed.

The intruder's boots paused, then pivoted. Butch pushed at Kiara to move her under the bed, but she resisted. When her expression turned fearful and she shook her head, he gave her a forceful shove and slid beside her in the narrow space with surprising speed and strength for a man so old.

The back of her head grazed against the underbelly of the bed. So little room. So confined. Butch patted her shoulder and offered a reassuring smile, but she felt her lungs lock down and her heartbeat accelerate.

"Relax," Butch said. "Breathe. Slowly. In and out. Steady. But stay silent. He's coming."

The intruder remained strangely quiet as he moved toward the bed. Not even the softest sigh of a footstep reached her impeccably attuned ears.

Kiara held her breath as he stopped at her bedside. She had the sudden urge to grab his ankles, like a real monster under the bed. She bet his boots would thud and squeak as he jumped away, giving him a taste of the terror he was trying to inflict upon her. But Butch clasped her hand in his wrinkled fingers. She frowned, irritated she would not get the satisfaction.

A hiss and rustle of sheets filled the air, followed by a few pillows falling onto the floor. Then she heard him flipping through the book she had fallen asleep reading, yet another history on Leonardo da Vinci. The intruder sighed and stepped back.

He strode to the center of her room and knelt. Slowly, he lifted the hatch door off the floor. Light beaconed from the hole, blasting the chandelier directly above and causing the crystal pieces to refract like tiny stars skittering about the room.

He wore no cloak now, only dark pants, a hoodie, and gloves.

In one fluid motion, he dropped through the hatch too quickly to have used the ladder. There was no thud from an impact below.

"How is he doing that?" Kiara whispered. "Maybe he's a ghost."

Giddiness fluttered over her skin, helping abate her initial panic, but she quickly crawled out from under the bed and rolled onto her back, happy for the open space. She sucked in deep breaths and worked to calm her racing heart.

Butch scooched out and stood, tucking the flannel shirt into his jeans and smoothing his sparse grey hair back before readjusting the cowboy hat back onto his head. Kiara smiled. Even in moments of danger, he liked to keep a neat appearance.

The delicate material of her nightgown clung to her small, slender body, but under her pale skin was a mass of sinewy muscle. She had delicate features, fine bones. The classic, serene beauty of a high society debutante in her late teens or early twenties. But looks could be deceiving.

Butch rolled his eyes. "If he was a ghost, why would he have opened the doors?"

"Good point." Flipping the long French braid of her dark hair over her shoulder, Kiara army-crawled for the hatch. "Do you think he knows he broke into the Palace of the Undead? How stupid do you have to be? We've got every kind of walking corpse imaginable down there. All hungry."

"Not stupid a'tall." His southern drawl came out harder in stress filled moments. "It would take weeks of research and surveillance, not to mention skill, to get in here." Butch leaned his frail body against the heaviest dresser and made an unsuccessful attempt to move it. "Close the hatch and lock it. Quietly. We'll put this over it."

"Or we can follow him. Quietly."

Kiara peered over the edge of the hatch. An orange-gold light warmed Leontes' library beneath, but she did not see the intruder.

"No, no, no." Butch rushed to stop her.

"Too late!"

Kiara hurried down the ladder, mindful of the books stacked on the steps. She was far too curious and bored to play it safe. Mostly bored. Being a ward of the Queen of the Undead was surprisingly uneventful.

The library was painfully empty. Bookcases were stuffed to their limits, with more volumes piled precariously on top. A polished wood desk overflowed with more books, a laptop, and papers. A case of scrolls hung open. Books and pillows were strewn all over the floor. Someone really needed to clean up after her before Leontes came home. He did not like things messy.

The bottom of the ladder leading down from her hatch opened up to four lanes between the chaotic jumble of bookcases. One path led to a heavy wooden door, the others to the far ends of the room where cozy sitting nooks awaited.

Kiara took a step toward the door, but Butch caught her arm and tugged her behind one of the bookcases. At her look, he put a finger to his lips and pointed. Through a bookshelf, she could see the hooded intruder tread out cautiously.

"Nice save, Butch," Kiara whispered. "Doesn't he look like Leontes?"

Butch gripped her arm to keep her from stepping out. "That is not your guardian."

"I know."

She could not see the intruder's face, but his hoodie was too large for his slender frame. His head came almost to the top of the towering bookcases, much like her guardian's did. The intruder clutched a syringe in his lithe fingers. A big one. It contained a dark liquid with shiny flecks swirling within.

That looked ominous. And deadly. Not something Leontes would have. Nor a thief. But an assassin would.

The man paused at the table behind the ladder. His shoulders shook with a short huff of a laugh. Mocking. He picked up a pen off a stack of papers. A quick scribble later, he moved around the table and headed their way.

Kiara hooked her arm through Butch's bony one and dragged him down the aisle. She slid around the bookcase, and when the old cowboy balked, she left him behind to rush down to the other end to follow the assassin.

She paused a moment. Risked a peek. The intruder's focus was on the door to the stairs down the tower. Kiara smiled. That would keep him busy for a while. It was locked from the outside. Kiara knew there was no way he could get through it since she had not been able to do so for over a month.

She darted out to the table behind the ladder. From the safety of the bookshelves, Butch waved his hands frantically. She ignored him and chose, instead, to stay and see what the stranger had found so interesting.

Case files. On Oleander.

It seemed everyone was brushing up on the ruthless serial killer and his modern-day murder spree. He had been dormant for hundreds of years, but the recent eruption of slayings had forced Kiara's guardian out of retirement. And out of her life for the last five weeks. She blinked against the sudden water in her eyes. She missed Leontes. Terribly.

"Focus," Butch whispered.

"Right, right," Kiara muttered.

The pen he had used sat atop the tally of Oleander's newest victims. The assassin had drawn a slash through it and sprawled a new number beneath, increasing it by over a hundred and adding the ominous words *"and counting"* at the end.

Kiara shivered with a sudden chill.

Metal moaned softly. She jumped. The assassin threw his back into opening the oak door. The vault-like attachment built into the opposite side of the wood and the solid steel lining made it heavier than it looked. Without sparing a glance back, the intruder slipped out, tucking the syringe in his pocket.

"Oh my God!" Kiara skirted around the desk after him. "He opened the door!"

"Kiara, stop." Butch stood in front of the exit, arms out. "I don't think he's here to steal anything."

"Neither do I." Kiara grinned at him as she passed by.

A quick check out the door revealed nothing but the man's shadow across the tight spiral of stairs. The stone steps were freezing against her bare feet, but Kiara hardly noticed, so excited at being out of the tower.

Butch kept a firm grip on Kiara's elbow to keep her from rushing down. The stairs opened up to a hall of eggshell-colored stone walls and creamy marble floors that were not any kinder to her feet.

Twisted iron chandeliers cast a bluish-white light on the intruder as, mid-step, he flicked his arms down and out to the side. Two short swords slid out from his sleeves. Without breaking stride, he sauntered out the end of the hall and swung his arms wide. Two heads toppled at his feet.

The assassin made a sharp left out of sight. In his wake, two bodies crumpled across the entryway on top of each other.

"Retreat!" Butch hissed.

Kiara sprinted ahead. "I think he's Oleander."

"So do I!" Butch screeched, eyes wild with fear. "Let's hide, missy. Now!"

"Let's go to the ocean!" Kiara flattened her back against the wall of the entryway, and then peeked out to make sure the coast was clear.

She spared only a casual glance at the dead bodies on the floor. Rotted faces and skin a sickly blotch of yellow and purple. An obsidian ooze glugged from their necks and stained the shiny marble. A couple of murdered zombies were certainly nothing to cry over. There were at least a few dozen more stumbling about the palace to replace them.

Out in the corridor, Butch twirled an anxious circle on the other side of the zombies. "The ocean? What about the serial killer loose in a palace full of potential victims?"

Kiara shrugged, skipped over the corpses, and headed the opposite way of the man she was now almost certain was Oleander. "Someone else's problem. Besides, you just said we should hide."

"Kiara," Butch growled.

"Ugh." Kiara let her head fall back with the groan. "Fine." She kicked a frustrated jig, then stomped after the assassin.

"Wait! I didn't mean *go after* Oleander." Butch fell in step beside her. "Just tell someone he's here."

Kiara smiled with anxious hope. "Then we go to the beach?"

"Yes. Wait!" He grabbed her arm to keep her from rounding the corner.

Kiara peeked out. The assassin stalked down the corridor and descended the stairs to the assembly room below. She waited a beat and then followed. The corridor also served as a balcony to view the large chamber below. Its black leather furniture was strangely empty. Usually, at least a few undead could be found hanging out there. The ebony curtains were drawn shut even though dawn was hours away.

"You know, we haven't heard a single sound since we got out," Butch said.

"So?"

"It's night and hundreds of undead live within these walls."

Kiara stilled and did a slow spin. "You're right. Where did they all go?"

Footsteps echoed up the stairs.

Kiara dropped on all fours and crawled under an accent table, rattling the vase of lilies perched on top.

Butch frowned. "Genius. No one will see the girl in the bright yellow nightgown."

"I don't have many options, do I?"

"A little magic would be extremely useful right about now."

"Very funny. Would you just hide before someone sees us?"

"Kiara?" a deep voice boomed.

"Ugh," Kiara groaned. "Busted."

CHAPTER 5

BANE STOOD A FEW PACES AWAY, several suited bodyguards at his flanks. He was a giant of a man, tall and thick, an intimidating mass of muscle. Despite the paleness of being a vampire for centuries, his skin was still dark enough to make evident his mixed-race ancestry. The bastard son of a French nobleman and his Haitian slave was all Kiara remembered, and she did not know how she knew that much. He was also the queen's right-hand man, although Kiara found little right about him.

Bane's midnight blue silk dress shirt stretched ever so subtly across his torso, just in case anyone failed to notice his immense size. He hitched his black trousers and scratched his heavy beard, which was always neatly trimmed.

"Bane!" Kiara rushed toward him.

Bane scowled in irritation. "What are you doing out of your cage, you tiny twit?" He patted the top of her head, easy to do since he towered at least a foot taller.

Kiara knocked his hand away. "You're a stupid . . . nitwit."

"Excuse me?" Bane raised a warning brow.

Butch pinched Kiara's arm.

"Fine." She rolled her eyes. "There's an intruder sneaking about the house. I think it's Oleander, and I think he came to kill me. You'd better call more guards."

Now it was Bane's turn to roll his eyes. "Great. Brain still on meltdown, little one?" He sighed. "So much for Dr. Lyons and all his useless hours. I'd be much more useful helping get your memory back."

"That's against the rules," Kiara said.

"So is breaking out of your room," he countered. "If Oleander really was here, there'd be no slinking quietly through the corridors." His smile turned dark. "The Butcher of Britain. The Flayer of France. Europe's finest executioner. Slaughtering entire villages—men, women, children—with so many slices of the scythe. Oleander always makes a splash. With gallons of blood and piles of body parts." He made a dramatic gesture of wiping away a fake tear. "I really miss those days."

"You miss killing?" Kiara asked.

"I miss the excitement of the unknown," Bane said wistfully. "The world has become such a bore. We should spar again, you and I. That always cheers me up."

"Doesn't cheer me up. Last time you gave me a black eye."

"Exactly," he smiled. "And the time before that, I gave you two black eyes *and* broke your arm. You should be thanking me."

"Why?"

"Because it shows you're improving, little one. With my help. How else are you going to learn? Leontes won't spar with you. He just plays stupid kid's games, like hide and seek." He shook his head with disdain.

"I don't think they're stupid," Kiara said.

"Because you're not right in the head. So, you and me, in the gym tomorrow? Let's say around—" He stopped to sniff the air and frowned. "Why do I smell zombie blood? What did you do now? I am not cleaning up another one of your messes."

"It wasn't me. It was the assassin."

"Of course it was," he said, thoroughly annoyed. "So what is it tonight? Another bad dream? Or are you hallucinating again?"

"Lie," Butch said.

"No." Kiara gave Bane a formal salute. "My mind is fit as a fiddle."

Kiara winked at Butch. He groaned.

Bane glanced at Kiara's side and shook his head. "Who is it this time? The old cowboy? He is a favorite of yours. You should hallucinate someone handsome and charismatic like me rather than that old fart."

"Hey!" Butch said, highly offended, then muttered, "Well, ain't no matter. Don't care what a dumb Sasquatch like him thinks anyway."

"Sure you don't," Kiara said.

"No sass from you, missy." Butch gave her an anxious glance. "And don't look at me. I'm not real!"

Kiara scratched her head. Sometimes that was hard to remember. Butch was a hallucination, conjured from some part of her fractured mind. Kiara breathed deep and focused on Bane.

"Where is everyone?" she asked.

"Charity ball." Bane's voice took an oddly tight lilt.

"Awesome." Kiara clapped her hands and grinned. "Let's go catch the assassin before they all get back. He can't be far. You just passed him on the stairs."

When Bane laid his left hand on her shoulder, Kiara stiffened. She would rather he did not touch her at all, let alone with the hand missing a digit. Only a heavily scarred nub remained where his ring finger should be. It gave Kiara the creeps.

He bowed low so he could look her in the eyes. "Look, little one, there was no one on the stairs and there's no scent out of the ordinary. You're having another bad night. That new medication Lyons prescribed is obviously useless."

Kiara slid Butch a sideways glance. "Are you sure the assassin is real?"

"Yes, but stop looking at me!" Butch backed out of view.

Kiara asked Bane, "Where's Frankie? Who's supposed to be watching me?"

"I am," Bane said. "Which isn't at all fair. I had to cancel a date to babysit the likes of you."

"Disappoint another supermodel? Or was it a starbet?" Kiara said. "You should be careful. I think one of your last dates was part fairy. The queen frowns on hanging out with the enemy. But you go ahead. I'll be fine."

"It's star*let*," he said with a lecherous smile. "Fairy? That would explain a few things. Now let's get you back to your room. I'll even tuck you in."

"Ew. No," Kiara cringed then backed away from Bane's touch. "Plus, it's against the rules, and Leontes wouldn't like it."

Bane shrugged. "Maybe not, but he's not here. And you know I hate rules."

"The queen left you with Bane?" Butch's voice was heavy with suspicion. "Something's wrong."

"I know," Kiara muttered. "Bane, help me catch him and you'll look good in front of the queen."

"I already look good," Bane smirked. "You're the one that needs to score points. Hey, if you want this killer so bad, go get him yourself."

Kiara narrowed her gaze. "You'd let me leave the mansion?"

"Sure. Because crazy is as crazy does, and if you want to prove you aren't crazy…" He stepped back and swept his arm down the hallway. "Have at it. I'm all about showing support."

"Sir," one of the guards said nervously. "That isn't sanctioned. I don't think—"

Bane slammed a fist into the man's face. The guard dropped flat on his back, unconscious, blood pouring from his nose. Another man started to help his comrade, but at Bane's steely look, the man put his hands behind his back and stared straight ahead.

Bane smiled at Kiara. "Go on, little one. Find this so-called intruder and prove everyone wrong." When Kiara hesitated, he added, "Unless you're really all talk. Don't actually have the guts to leave the mansion, eh? The Kiara I remember wouldn't be such a coward. But what do I know?" His smile widened, showing his fangs.

Kiara lifted her chin and threw back her shoulders in a defiant pose.

"No!" Butch cried. "Don't do it."

But Kiara ignored him and gathered her skirt. She strode past Bane and the guards, ready to jump out of the way if any of them tried to grab her.

They did not.

Bane gave a low chuckle that echoed off the stone walls. He told the guards, "Bring me the copper penny. I suddenly have an appetite."

Butch raced to catch up to Kiara. "You realize he just goaded you into this idiotic move, don't you? Bane never, I repeat *never*, has your best interests at heart. This is all kinds of bad. Leontes would not approve!"

"Like Bane said," Kiara shot back with heavy bitterness, "Leontes isn't here."

CHAPTER 6

KIARA PULLED ON A PAIR OF HEAVY BOOTS she kept hidden near the front door and ran outside. She took some time enjoying the smell of freedom before focusing on the intruder's scent, following it through the various modern buildings and into the woods that surrounded the compound.

The sprawling estate rambled over endless acres of rolling hills along the Malibu beach coastline. She easily skirted through the wilderness, unconcerned with the shrubs and branches that caught her nightgown. She headed away from the cliffs and the soothing sound of pounding surf. When she came to the high wall at the perimeter, she did not hesitate. In one great leap, she landed on top of it in a crouch, staring down at the road directly below.

"Kiara, don't do this," Butch pleaded from the ground.

"I'm not scared."

"That's the problem. You should be scared. You ain't equipped for this. You've been in that mansion for years. You don't know a thing of the outside world."

"That's what makes it so exciting!"

"No, it doesn't!"

She grinned. "Don't be such an old fart."

Out of sight, an engine roared to life. Kiara leapt down to the road and rushed toward the sound, but by the time she made it around the bend, the car was driving off. She ran, picking up speed, but the car pulled away.

Kiara slowed, and before the red taillights disappeared in the growing mist, she pointed her finger and said, "I will find you."

As the mist thickened into a drizzle, Butch appeared next to her, doubled over and wheezing. "And how are you going to do that? Stop the next vehicle and demand that they follow that car?"

"Great idea!"

Headlights came around a corner. From the side of the road, Kiara waved her arms. "Hello! Stop!"

"Quit that!" Butch yelled. "I was joking! This isn't like one of your movies!"

The car passed without slowing. The next two cars did the same, even though she tried various tactics. Smiling wide, sticking two thumbs up, showing them a peace sign, and even yanking up her skirt to show off her boots. When the third and fourth car came along, Kiara stomped several frustrated steps into the road, causing them to swerve and honk loudly, but they kept going.

"No one is going to stop on their own," Butch told her, looking up at the sky. "You look like a lunatic axe murderer. The rain is getting worse. You're getting soaked. It's time to go back."

"You're right," Kiara agreed.

"Finally." Butch turned back toward the mansion. "If we hurry, and if Bane keeps his mouth shut, no one will ever know that you left. Kiara? I said if we hurry…"

But Kiara was not listening. She chewed on her lip and, when the next set of headlights appeared, she walked into the middle of the road and stood in the rain, facing the oncoming car.

CHAPTER 7

THE ONLY THING LOUDER THAN THE SCREECH OF TIRES on wet pavement was the scream of the girl inside the car.

Skidding on the slick road, the car came closer and closer, fishtailing the final few yards as it headed straight for Kiara. At the last second, she slammed her hand down on the edge of the hood and brought the car to an abrupt halt that lifted the vehicle's rear end off the ground.

The tires landed back on the pavement with a pounding *thud*. Kiara rushed to the passenger side. The teenage girl's hands covered her face. Her screams subsided to shaky whimpers.

The young man in the driver's seat, with thick black-framed glasses askew on his face, had his eyes closed and his hands locked on the steering wheel as he muttered, "Oh my God, oh my God," over and over again.

Kiara knocked on the window.

Both occupants threw their hands in the air and shrieked.

Kiara cringed against the loud noise. She could smell their fear and adrenaline, hear their hearts pumping like jackhammers. She smiled in what she hoped was a reassuring manner and spoke calmly.

"Hello. Thank you for stopping. I could really use your help."

Eyes bugged, the girl stammered, "You-you-you're not dead?"

Kiara shrugged. "I'm a little dead. But that's a long story for another time." She opened the rear door and climbed into the backseat. "I need you to follow a car. I must apprehend an assassin."

The two teens stared at each other, then twisted around to stare at Kiara.

"What!" the girl said.

"Are you crazy?" cried the boy.

Kiara smiled. "Wow, you two are really killing it with the guesses tonight. But again, long story, another time. Now, if you wouldn't mind." She pulled something out of her boot and showed it to the two wide-eyed occupants. "I'm on a very important case, and we really need to go."

The boy stared at the gold badge and turned green. "Oh, God. I almost killed a cop."

CHAPTER 8

"**SHE'S CLIMBING OUT!** Jeez, Eddie. Out the roof. She's climbing out the roof!"

"What am I supposed to do, Daphne? I'm driving! Or trying to. She's letting the rain in, and it's getting on my glasses and I can hardly see! Why'd you let her open the moonroof anyway?"

"Because she's a cop! And I thought it was a sunroof."

"Not at night, duh." He took off his glasses and wiped them awkwardly on his jeans, then hunched over the wheel again, squinting through the smeared spectacles. "Get her back in here. But be careful. This car is vintage and my mom will freak if there's a scratch."

"It isn't vintage. It's just old. And getting her inside isn't so easy." Daphne grabbed at Kiara's swinging legs, almost getting kicked in the head as the 'detective' wiggled out. "Stop the car!"

"No!" Kiara said, plopping herself on the edge of the roof's opening, letting her booted feet dangle inside the car. "We must follow him. Stay on course. I can smell him better from out here."

"Did she say *smell* him?" Eddie said, his voice rising above accepted masculine levels.

They had been driving for a while, heading into Los Angeles, with Kiara giving directions. She stared at the city as they passed by.

Her body tingled with glorious excitement. So much life happening with shops and restaurants and humans doing dozens of different things. Laughing and talking, eating and drinking. She had seen a most colorful Ferris wheel turning round and round on the pier. There were even people dancing inside a place where music blared and vibrant lights flashed. If she were not tracking an assassin, she would love to stop and experience it all.

People on the street holding umbrellas stopped to point at her, then laughed and waved. Kiara grinned and waved back. This was so much better than watching stuff on movies and television. She might as well enjoy it a little. Who knew when she would get out again?

If she found Oleander, she would be a hero. It just might buy her some freedom.

"Are you kidding?" Butch said, shivering next to her in the cold rain. "They're gonna chain you to the bed once they have you again. Or put you back in a coffin."

"Shut up," Kiara said, still waving and trying not to let him kill her good mood. A few cars honked at her. Feeling like a princess in a parade, she waved at them, too.

"I'm telling you, badge or no badge, something's not right." Eddie wiped his glasses again and squinted through the frantic windshield wipers. "I think she's an alien. Or a superhero. Or both."

"Wow, your nerd is really showing." Daphne took his glasses, wiped them dry with her shirt, and then handed them back to Eddie. "She told you there was a big fallen branch in the road that you ran into. You've been to way too many comic cons."

"How many times do I have to tell you, there is only one *Comic Con?* The others are just pathetic attempts at imitating an original masterpiece."

"Sure. Nerd," she said with a playful grin. "Hey, I was thinking that maybe she could help you with your, you know, problem. She is a cop."

Eddie stiffened. "A strange cop. And no, don't say anything. I can handle it." He put his hand over hers. "But thanks."

Daphne looked like she wanted to protest, but instead, shielded her eyes from the rain and looked up at Kiara. "Aren't you cold? Why are you wearing a nightgown in the middle of a big murder case?"

"I'm undercover." Kiara smiled at her cleverness.

"In a nightgown?"

"I'm, uh, very undercover."

Butch groaned, "Oh, brother."

"Please, human," Kiara said. "No questions. It is for your own safety."

"Did she just call you *human?*" Eddie asked, his voice laced with a hint of nerdy excitement.

"You're making it worse," Butch said. "I told you not to engage. And if you won't go back to the mansion, we at least need to call Leontes. Wherever he is, he can send someone to help."

"I meant ma'am, and I don't have a phone," Kiara said quickly. It was difficult having two conversations.

"I have a phone." Daphne pulled one from her purse and held it up. "You need to call for backup, right?"

"Yes!" Butch shouted.

He was probably right. They were getting close to Oleander. But Kiara stared at the piece of equipment.

Butch shook his head. "Don't know how to use it, do you?"

Kiara glared at him, then said, "Excuse me Miss Daf-elbow, could you please—"

"Elbow? What are you talking about? Oh." The girl chuckled. "It's Daph*ne*, not elbow. And no 'Miss' in front. Just Daphne. You are so funny."

"So *weird*," Eddie said, then quickly whispered, "and not of this world."

"Yes, of course. Miss, I mean, just Daf-*knee*, would you please call my...superior." Kiara rattled off the number Leontes had given her for emergencies.

A few moments later, Daphne said, "Your lieutenant, or captain or whoever, isn't answering. I can text him. What do you want me to say?"

This could be tricky. "Say that it is Kiara, that I am perfectly fine, that I am out of the mansion—yes, please say mansion—and that I am with friends, and I am fine. Very fine."

"Okay, sent." Daphne smiled up at Kiara. "I also said that we were on the trail of an assassin and that you needed your LAPD backup pronto."

"Oh," Kiara said. "Please take that part back, because it probably wasn't a good—"

The phone rang. Daphne answered, but before she could get in a word the caller started shouting.

Kiara closed her eyes. "—idea."

CHAPTER 9

AT LEONTES' VEHEMENT INSISTENCE, they had pulled over and provided their location. While Kiara paced along the sidewalk and spoke on the phone, Daphne and Eddie leaned against the car.

"No, they are very nice, Leontes. They helped me, and I didn't even have to glamour them. I just showed them my badge."

"Badge?" Leontes said. "Oh, dear God. Detective Cage."

Kiara grinned. "At your service, Lieutenant Leontes. See, you don't have to worry."

"Worry!" he bellowed. "I am so far beyond worry, you have no bloody clue! Have you told them anything significant about who or what you are?"

"No, but for humans, they've got some really good guesses. Why didn't you tell me you were back?"

Eddie looked at Daphne with a knowing smile. "She called us humans again."

"I know."

"You know who calls people 'humans'?"

"Non-humans?"

"Non-hu— Exactly right."

Daphne shrugged. "I've read that when cops go deep undercover for a long time, they can go a little crazy."

"Oh, right, sure, makes sense because, what, she's been undercover in a witch's coven?"

Kiara laughed. "No, silly. Vampire, duh. But I am part witch. More of a sorceress, really. Although, I don't have any magical ability since I came out of the coffin. It's a—"

"Another long story." Daphne nodded. "We understand. Can't wait to hear it."

Eddie did a double take. "Okay, excuse me, what? She just used vampire, witch, sorceress, *and* coffin in the same sentence. Are you not hearing this?"

Daphne smirked. "She's just messing with you because she knows you are such a nerd."

"Kiara, stop talking!" Leontes sounded ready to burst through the phone.

"It's really okay," Kiara said. "I think nerd means someone who knows about supernatural stuff and is okay with it. So we're good."

"See." Daphne gave Eddie a smug smile and punched his shoulder. "Totally messing with you."

Kiara punched his shoulder, too. "Totally."

Eddie bounced off the car and fell flat on his butt, grabbing at his chest. "Ow! That hurt! Did you see that? She is fricking way too strong for normal."

"I'm so sorry." Kiara offered a hand, but Eddie scooted away.

Daphne rolled her eyes and helped him up. "Come on, wuss. I'm going to miss curfew if we don't hurry. Kiara, do you need us for anything else?"

"No!" Leontes shouted. "Get them out of there. I will arrive within minutes. Find somewhere to hide and talk to no one."

"But—"

"No one!"

"Fine. I have to give Daf-ankle back her phone."

The girl laughed. "Daph-ankle. You're a riot."

"How did you know?" Kiara said. "I did cause a riot once. Just for fun, because it gets so boring. I told the ghouls at the mansion that the zombies were talking behind their backs, and then the ghosts got involved and, holy moly, it was a blood bath. Not for the ghosts, because they don't bleed, of course, but—"

"Kiara!" Leontes yelled.

"Yes, sorry." She smiled tightly. "Goodbye, Leontes."

"No, do not hang up," he said quickly. "I do not want to lose you. I mean, the connection with you. Tell the girl I will pay her for the phone."

"Keep it," Daphne said. "I'm due for an upgrade anyway."

Kiara paused. "You're giving me a gift? But I have nothing for you. Oh, I know. I could curse you. It's my own family recipe."

"Whoa." Eddie grabbed Daphne's arm and pulled her back. "Thanks, but no thanks. We're good. Really. Fine and dandy. Sweet of you to offer, but a serious no on the cursing."

Daphne shrugged off Eddie's grip and patted Kiara's shoulder. "Just be careful. And promise you'll call and let me know how it all goes down. You can tell us one of those long stories when we hang out again." She scribbled on a piece of paper she took from her purse. "Here's my address."

"Hang out?" Kiara asked, taking the paper, her eyes suddenly misty. "Yes, thank you. I would very much like that. I have much gratitude for your assistance, Sir Edward."

Daphne said, "Not sir, and it's just—"

"No." Eddie pushed his glasses up his nose. "Sir Edward works."

Daphne snorted, then pulled Kiara into a hug. Kiara stiffened for a moment. She could not remember the last time anyone hugged her. Unless you counted the headlocks Bane put her in when they sparred. But she did not think so. Those did not feel good. Not like this, which sent a warmth spreading through her whole body. Kiara smiled and wrapped her arms around the girl.

Daphne grunted. "Oh, wow. Eddie's right. You are strong."

Kiara let her go and moved toward Eddie with her arms open. He took a quick step back and waved from a wary distance, then both he and Daphne got in the car. As they drove off, Daphne yelled out the window, "Shouldn't you have a gun?"

Kiara waved. "I should totally have a gun. Leontes—"

"No guns."

She started to roll her eyes, but a strong scent suddenly carried over the breeze, causing her to catch breath. Fresh blood. A lot of it.

"Oh no," Kiara whispered. "He's killing again."

CHAPTER 10

THE DRIZZLE CONTINUED. Dark clouds dragged across the moon as Kiara raced through the neighborhood and came to a stop in front of a large house set far back from the street behind an electronic security gate. There were no lights on inside or out. The luxury exterior of the home contradicted the perfume of fear, blood, and death wafting from within.

A rising wind fluttered her dress in wet slaps against her legs as Kiara gave Leontes the new address.

"For God's sake," he demanded through the phone. "I am telling you— no, ordering you, for the final time, to stop and wait for me, and *do not hang up.* You know the rules. You cannot be out, let alone unsupervised."

"But the assassin is inside."

"If there even is an assassin! The house could be full of innocent humans."

Kiara flinched. He thought she was hallucinating. The sting of that realization flushed her cheeks. But Butch had said the killer was real. Where was Butch? A quick glance around revealed he had abandoned her.

Through the phone, Kiara heard the screech of tires as Leontes squealed around a corner on his race to get to her. She said, "You're such a worry wart. I've been out for hours and nothing's gone wrong. What's the worst that could happen?"

Gunshots shattered the silence of the night. Bright flashes of light lit the interior of the house.

"What was that?"

"Good," Kiara said with relief. "You heard it, too."

In one fluid motion, she leapt over the gate and ran for the porch. The splintered front door hung drunkenly on one hinge.

"Automatic gunfire. Inside." Kiara fought to stay calm. She needed to focus. Wet from the rain, she brushed back the dark tendrils tangling across her eyes and took deep breaths, the smell of gunpowder strong.

"No. Kiara, whatever happens, do *not* go inside the—"

Kiara eased off the clunky, muddied boots and hopped barefoot over the door onto the cold tile. "I'm in the house."

"Goddammit!" His words disintegrated into a groan. "Kiara? Wait for me outside!"

Kiara poked her head into the living room. Through the rain-spattered windows, the hazy glow from streetlights filtered in to chase at shadows crawling the walls. Three lawn chairs and a card table sat empty in a room which was otherwise devoid of furniture. She smelled the ravaged flesh and the coppery scent of spilled blood before she saw the bodies.

Seven well-muscled men, faces frozen in a final grimace, lay crumpled on the floor, limbs at odd angles, blood pooling beneath them. Automatic guns lay scattered a few feet away, the metal bent as if it had been heated and warped.

Or twisted by a tremendous amount of brute force.

The dead bodies did not faze her, but the black flower petals on the ground and the symbol on the wall stole her breath. Two scythes, crisscrossed at the handles, were painted in blood, the crimson lines dripping in a macabre fashion.

"Leontes, it's Oleander. His death crest is drawn in blood above two corpses." Kiara tiptoed to the wall, careful to keep from stepping in the spreading pools of red. She tilted her head and wrinkled her nose. "There's a business card. Stuck on the wall with blood."

Leontes cursed. "Do not look at the card. Leave it alone."

Kiara peeled the card off the wall with a sticky, wet crackle. Oleander's death crest took center stage on the front of the glossy white card. On the back, spiked vines with vibrant red blossoms entwined around a clear glass jar filled with thick scarlet liquid. Thanks to an infusion of magic, the bottle appeared real. Like a 3-D hologram. As Kiara moved the card, the potion inside the container swirled and glowed.

She released a weary sigh.

Leontes' flat voice crackled the silence. "Let me guess. You looked at the card."

"It's the Midnight Poison," Kiara said. "Which means all this killing has to do with me, doesn't it? Why didn't you say something?"

"We do not know that for certain."

"Yeah, right. Just because I don't remember doesn't mean I'm stupid."

"Of course not," Leontes said with growing tension. "I simply did not want to—"

"Send me off the deep end?"

"No. I did not want to involve you until I had more facts."

"And more dead bodies."

She shut the dead men's eyes, then wiped her bloodied fingers on the skirt of her rain-soaked nightgown. That was better. Sort of. She was not fond of dead things. Especially ones that seemed to stare at her with accusing eyes.

Above her, the floorboards groaned.

She spun, dress fanning out, hair flinging water droplets to mix with the blood that spattered the wall. "He's upstairs!"

In a voice that shook as he fought for control, Leontes said, "Kiara, trust me when I say you are out of your depth here. Get out now. Please."

He was probably right. And it made her angry. She turned to leave when movement caught her attention. She twirled on the balls of her feet, ready for the worst.

End of Excerpt